My School Musical and other Punishments

CATHERINE WILKINS

nosy crow

First published in the UK in 2014 by Nosy Crow Ltd
The Crow's Nest, 10a Lant Street
London, SE1 1QR, UK

Nosy Crow and associated logos are trademarks and/or registered
trademarks of Nosy Crow Ltd

Text © Catherine Wilkins, 2014
Cover illustration © Sarah Horne, 2014
Interior illustrations © Sarah Horne, 2014

A CIP catalogue record for this book is available from the British Library

Printed and bound in the UK by Clays Ltd, St Ives Plc
Typeset by Tiger Media Ltd, Bishops Stortford, Hertfordshire

Papers used by Nosy Crow are made from wood grown in
sustainable forests.

ISBN: 978 0 85763 309 5

www.nosycrow.com

For just Rich.

Happy now?

C. W.

Chapter 1

"Can I tell you about my brilliant idea now?" I ask. "I'm kind of on a time limit here." I'm pretty sure I've managed to phrase this politely rather than arrogantly.

"Hah. *Arrogant much?*" laughs Joshua. Then again, maybe I haven't.

Sometimes I find it tiring being a genius. (By the way, I know I may not be a genius *yet*, but I read somewhere that you have to *act as if.*)

I attempt to be more tactful. "It's just we keep having the same old arguments about whether to put the price of the comic up, and I have to be—"

"Rules is rules, Toons," interrupts Tanya Harris. She then indicates the pad of paper on her lap, as if it's the sacred word of law, rather than a manifesto for a cheeky comic about our school made up by four eleven-year-olds.

I think it's a bit rich Tanya telling me *rules is rules*, when she used to be the naughtiest and scariest girl in our school up until about five minutes ago (practically).

Which *rule* was she obeying when she spat in Mrs Cole's face, I wonder? Or when she kept putting chewing gum in Amelia's hair? *Exactly.* (I'm not about to ask her this though, I'm not *insane*. She's still a tiny bit terrifying, even though she's now a "businesswoman".)

But I don't have time for all this – I need to get back to my form room to stop Amelia doing something I will regret. Or to help her not do it. What I mean is, I have to stop her from making another huge mistake which will ultimately be very helpful of me. We need a new word that means stop and help. Stelp? I need to *stelp* Amelia. **STELP**

"We all have other things going on," says Joshua. "The school-musical auditions are tomorrow – I could be going over my lines, or practising."

"Are you … *auditioning?*" I can't really hide my surprise.

"Yes," replies Joshua.

"*Really?*" I guess I sound incredulous.

"*Yes!*" repeats Joshua crossly.

It's just I never really had Joshua down as an all-singing, all-dancing kind of guy. He's always acting like he's so cool and above everything. His tall aloofness, constant eyebrow-raising and being on the school basketball team made me assume he wouldn't necessarily want to be in *The Wizard of Oz*. I mean, he loves *comics*, for goodness' sake! (Starting our own was his idea.)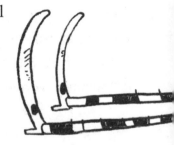

"Jessica, you're the one making this take way longer than it needs to," interrupts Lewis. The voice of reason, as ever. Pedantic and shy, Lewis is also good at drawing cartoons. He and I do pretty much all the drawing.

I want to be a cartoonist when I grow up, like my hero Matt Groening. Or, at least, some kind of artist who draws things. Anyway, that's not important right now. Must stop being distracted by my own brilliant mind. Hmm, maybe Lewis is right. I *am* dragging it out a bit.

"OK, OK," I say. "Sorry. Can we move on to new ideas?"

"No," says Tanya. "We're still on Any Other Business."

I sigh and look at my watch. They're probably voting *right now*. My best friend, Natalie; my best … frenemy, Amelia; Cassy, all those other—

"So!" booms Tanya. "Any Other Business?" Silence. "OK, on to new ideas."

Finally. "Right," I say.

"Wait," instructs Tanya.

"For *what*?" I ask.

"Does anyone have any new ideas?" asks Tanya.

"Yes! *I* do!" I say, frantically.

Tanya bursts out laughing. "You're well easy to wind up, Toons. Classic. You should see your face!"

Joshua and Lewis look annoyingly amused as well. Part of me wants to storm out of the Quiet Reading Area, but the bigger part of me is trying not to laugh.

"Hilarious," I say dryly.  BRILLIANT

"Come on then, let's hear it," smiles Joshua. "Let's hear this amazing, fantastic idea of yours."

"For the record, I only said it was brilliant," I say. "But I can't help it if *all* my ideas are brilliant. It can be lonely up here, at the top, being brilliant all the time."

Joshua chuckles. Lewis frowns and says, "I thought you were in a hurry?"

Oh, *I am. Amelia!* I snap back to attention. "OK. My idea is called *The Parents' Handbook.* It's kind of like a jokey *do's and don'ts* for parents. Like:  'Always give your children sweets, it makes them happy.' It's basically the opposite of what my parents do do." (*Ha ha – I said "doo-doo".*)

"That is actually a pretty good idea," says Joshua, as a grin spreads across his face.

"Love it!" cries Tanya. "Done it again, Toons! Knocked it out the park, innit."

"I think it has comic potential," Lewis adds more sedately.

"It could even be a series!" enthuses Joshua. "We could do all sorts of other ones like, *The Teachers' Handbook*, or—"

"*The Being Cool Handbook*," interjects Tanya.

"Yeah!" agrees Joshua.

"*Teachers' Handbook:* item one," I joke. "Don't interrupt pupils when they are talking."

The others laugh. I *love* it when they laugh at my jokes. And when we all build on each other's ideas like this. We're a really good team (you know, apart from all the arguments).

"Hey, maybe we could all work together on it?" says Joshua. I glance at my watch again.

"Sure," I say. "But at the next meeting, I really have to go now." And then I scarper away and pelt towards my form room.

$\Longrightarrow$

"OK, what did I miss?" I say, as I arrive, **6C** panting, at our desks in 6C.

"Uh, try *everything*?" Amelia replies disdainfully.

"You missed the vote, Jess." Natalie smiles sadly at me.

"Oh *God*." I moan, putting my head in my hand. Then I look back up at them. "What are we?"

"We're the 'Discerning Awesome Fit Team'," replies Emily. The – what? *Nooooooo!*

"I added the *fit*," says Amelia's snooty friend, Cassy, proudly. "I think it's important to be healthy. And pretty." She smiles.

I can't help myself. "You **IDIOTS!** idiots!" I blurt out.

"Um, *hello*?" snaps Amelia. "For your information, *discerning* means *intelligent*, so we most certainly are *not* idiots."

"But don't feel bad that we know more words than you," adds Cassy smugly, making her and Amelia chuckle.

"It spells out *DAFT*!" I cry. "You've re-named our gang DAFT. You absolutely *are* idiots. I *told* you, whatever you choose, make sure the initials don't spell something stupid!"

"Well," Amelia pauses, looking uncomfortable for a moment. "You don't say it DAFT, you say it D.A.F.T." **D.A.F.T**

⇨

"It's not that bad, Jess," says Natalie, as people start moving back to their own desks at the end of lunch.

"And we gave you *plenty* of warning about the meeting," adds Amelia huffily. "You were the one that kept complaining about the old name. If you cared so much, you should have come to it."

Honestly. I have to do *everything* myself. This is what happens if I am not around to babysit everyone every two minutes.

I sigh loudly as the remaining members of DAFT trail back to their own classroom. DAFT, formerly known as GUF. Formerly *formerly* known as ACE and CAC.

Spot the name *I* came up with. *ACE.* (I thank you.) It stood for Awesome Cool Enterprises because *I* understand how acronyms work. And Amelia – despite being one of the top in the class – still doesn't.

I *knew* I should have been here. I knew I couldn't trust them to at least *check* what it spelled out before they voted. Amelia's track record speaks for itself. Leaving aside for a moment the fact that she originally only started a secret gang with Natalie to deliberately exclude *me*, her name choices have always been terrible.

First she came up with Cool Awesome Chicks, or CAC (which I've always said made it sound like one of the milder swear words for poo). Then, when we buried the hatchet and merged our two warring gangs of ACE (which I had started to get back at them) and CAC, she named it Great United Friends, or GUF. (I missed that meeting, too.) So then we sounded like a gang of fart clouds.

I suppose at least we do seem to have moved away from poo and smelling like it, and into a new arena of general stupidity. Maybe I *should* be grateful.

"Yeah, maybe it's not too bad," I lie. I don't want her to feel bad for being a party to this tomfoolery. She was probably distracted anyway, thinking about her audition for the school musical. She's been very focused on that lately.

And the rest of the nice ACE gang all have reasons not to point it out. Cherry and Shantair, my chess-club friends, are clever enough to have spotted the whole DAFT pitfall, but they don't care enough about the gang thing to be bothered. In fact, they sort of think it's all a bit stupid but harmless.

My other friends, Emily, Megan and Fatimah (who I sit with in Art and French) just mess about most of the time. They're always getting told off for talking in class. So they probably didn't even notice what was happening.

But Amelia's snooty, super-cool friends like Cassy all pride themselves on their academic excellence. They think there are two things in life that are really brilliant: (1) being clever, and (2) knowing about fashion. So they totally *should* have noticed.

But no doubt they were so busy showing off because they knew the word *discerning,* and then desperately trying to crowbar in the word *fit*, they missed what was staring them in the face. And yet they say *I'm* the idiot.

Chapter 2

"Oh my God, next time you see me, I'm going to be auditioning!" Natalie gives me a massive hug as I stand up to get off the bus after school. It's slightly disconcerting.

"Well, there's a whole morning of lessons tomorrow first," I say. "And presumably I'll see you then?"

"You know what I mean! I'm so nervous. I don't think I'm going to get any sleep tonight!"

"You'll be brilliant," I say firmly, then disembark and head towards my house.

I hear the new dog barking as I put my key in the front door. *Yay! The new dog!* I *love* the new dog. *Everyone* does. Well, my mum maybe not so much. Everyone *else*.

OMG!

Though, actually, I think my mum does love the new dog *now*, but she sort of went through this stage where she kept saying, "We are absolutely not keeping it." But I mean, that's open to interpretation, right? (Ha ha, I am funny.)

What happened was this: my older sister Tammy (who's already left home to be a student) and my crazy (in a mainly fun way) Auntie Joan turned up at our house one day with a rescued dog.

Tammy had been threatening to do this for ages. She's very into saving things. And I think Auntie Joan's *act now, think later* spirit finally tipped her into action.

I'm pretty sure the only reason my mum let them over the threshold and into the house *at all* was so we could argue in the privacy of the living room instead of out in the street in front of the neighbours.

So we all sat in the living room while the dog sat panting and wagging its tail at us. With its mouth open so it kind of looked like it was smiling.

"We are absolutely *not* keeping this dog," said my mum. "Let me tell you that right now."

"I completely agree with your mother," my dad said. Then, optimistically, "Maybe we could call him Bilbo?"

"It's a girl," said Tammy.

"Lady," said my little brother, Ryan.

"Yes, lady, whatever," said Tammy.

"No, we could *call* her Lady," explained Ryan.

We all looked at the dog. Despite panting loudly with her tongue lolling out of her mouth she did have a sort of haughty, regal look about her. She held her head quite high, so it was a bit like she was looking down on us. And she was all golden because she was a mixture of a collie and a golden retriever.

Then she rolled over and Ryan started patting her stomach. She loved that, you could tell. She started rolling around like a crazy thing, then sat up again, licked Ryan's hand, and laid her head mournfully in his lap, gazing up at him.

"I love you, Lady," said Ryan. Then he looked at my mum with tears in his little six-year-old eyes, and added, "Please don't take her away."

I remember thinking: *Well played, Lady, well*

played. So really it was Dog: 1, Mum: 0 from the off.

I really wanted to keep the dog, too. But I didn't want my mum to be upset either. She's mainly a really nice person. You know, really nice *for a mum*. Like, she only spoils all my fun *some* of the time. Which is pretty generous, if you think about it.

She tends to be a bit angrier than the mums you see on yoghurt adverts, but luckily my dad can usually calm her down with a cup of tea.

"It's me. Lady, you can stop barking now," I say pointlessly, as I open the front door.

Lady always barks when someone comes to the house. She is a brilliant guard dog in this way. Except, once you open the door, she stops barking and just wags her tail loads because she's so pleased to see you.

So, Lady is a great guard dog if you think that burglars would be terrified of her wagging her tail at them. Maybe if they had cynophobia? (That's a fear of dogs, fact fans.) But if they did,

they probably wouldn't choose to be burglars in the first place, I'm guessing.

I stroke Lady's head, and she sits down in my way so I can stroke her more. "Nice try, Lady, but I'm not staying here all day, stroking you," I tell her. Oh well, maybe just for a minute.

Lady had already had a couple of litters of puppies when she was found, living as a stray. But she was neutered at the dog's home so, much to mine and Ryan's disappointment, she can't have any more puppies.

And she's totally safe for us to have around. She's surprisingly well trained for a previously wild animal. She sits on command, loves playing with us and is completely housetrained.

The only slight issue is the whole chewing-stuff thing. But I'm sure that's just a phase. Like when my dad wanted to grow his own tomatoes, or when mum said we had to take our shoes off as soon as we came into the house.

I finally side-step Lady and make it to the kitchen, where my mum is putting together the finishing touches to macaroni cheese, with *Super Saver Value* pasta and

Super Saver Value cheese. My dad has just made her a cup of tea.

"*And*," says my dad, not yet noticing me, "I saw eight *more* birds at the bird feeder just *now*. It's a real hit with them, I tell you."

"Great." My mum sounds completely uninterested.

"And I think you and I can both agree that the new energy-saving light bulbs that Horace recommended have definitely been a success. He's just great, you know. I check his website daily now. It feels good to be doing something to help the planet again."

"Oh hello, Jess," says my mum. "Your dad has had some very good news today."

"Eight birds at the bird feeder? Epic," I say, faintly sarcastically, as I sit down at the table.

My mum ignores me and addresses my dad. "This is nearly ready. Where's Ryan?"

"I last saw him in the living room with Lady," replies my dad. "He was turning the sofa cushions into a spaceship again."

(My little brother is obsessed with space travel.)

"*Oh*," my mum sighs, annoyed. "Well, why didn't you stop him?"

"He looked so happy," answers my dad.

"Terrific," mutters my mum. "Left to old *muggins here* to sort everything out as usual."

Great, I see she's still trying to set up the nickname "muggins". Maybe I can finally put a stop to this by giving her a different, *better* nickname?

I clear my throat. "What's up? What's the news, *Big Mama*?" I say confidently.

"What the *heck* did you just call me?" My mum spins round and stares at me, bewildered.

Then again, maybe not. "OK, not that one. There are other ones we can go with," I reply amicably.

My mum shakes her head then turns away from me, draining the pasta over the sink. I can just hear mutterings of, "Haven't got time for this… Don't know what's *wrong* with everyone… It's the *living end*."

"I was trying to give you a nickname," I explain.

"Well, I don't need a nickname," Mum replies. *Finally*.

"What could my nickname be?" asks my dad,

suddenly interested.

"Um, well, you like helping the environment and birds," I say. "So how about, and this is just off the top of my head, how about … *The Environator*?"

My parents both stare at me for a moment.

"We're not doing that," says my mum.

"I can come up with better ones than that," I say quickly. "And there's no judgment in blue sky."

"*Anyway*," says my mum, brightening. "We have fantastic news. Jessica, your dad has had a pay rise and we are out of the economy drive!"

"What?! That's properly amazing!" I say, nearly jumping up. And ha! My mum has admitted that we *were* still on an economy drive after all, even though they claimed we were just "tightening our belts".

The distinction is this: "economy drive" = Mum will not buy food until we have used up everything in the freezer and cupboards (including defrosting a bit of their twenty-year-old wedding cake for "dessert"

one time). "Tightening our belts" = Mum will only buy food from the "reduced-to-clear" section at the supermarket or from the *Super Saver Value* range.

To be fair, it was mainly fine, though some bits were worse than others. (Let's just say I am definitely not a fan of *Super Saver Value* Spam fritters.) And my mum herself admitted that if you had to use two *Super Saver Value* tea bags per cup instead of one, it was a slightly flawed enterprise.

Ryan was pretty devastated about the lack of KitKats under this regime. But now it sounds like all our favourite branded snacks are back! We can officially move up from *Super Saver Value* brand crisps to *supermarket* brand crisps. *Result*. We've gone up one whole social class. Next stop: *Walkers*; then onwards, to Buckingham Palace.

"Congrats, Dad!" I say.

"Yes," says my dad, looking wistful. "Yes, it is good news," he adds glumly. That kind of seems like an *odd* reaction.

"Um… You don't sound very excited," I comment.

"He *is* very excited," asserts my mum.

"He doesn't completely sound … that happy," I say.

"Oh no, I am happy and excited," insists my dad unconvincingly. "It's good news, of course it's good news. It will be a new, big challenge and … responsibility and…" He sighs.

"And what?" I ask.

"It's just, um, lately I suppose I've been thinking about how I ended up in a job like this, when all I ever wanted to do was be like Horace King."

"Oh, not *this* again," says my mum crossly.

Last year as part of the class wildlife project, we had to write letters to environment-type people. I wrote to Horace King (my dad's childhood hero and now doddery old environmentalist and bird enthusiast who is still sometimes on telly teaching people how to make the aforementioned bird feeders).

Because Horace loved my letter, Nat, my dad and I got to meet him. My dad was over the moon at the time. But after the excitement faded, and he was back to normal daily life, he's been… Well, I guess it kind of changed him a bit.

"Come on, Bert," says my mum kindly but firmly. "You know we can't always get exactly what we want. I wanted to be a forensic scientist." (*Did she? Blimey.*) "But you don't hear *me* complaining." (*Well*, we don't hear her complaining *about that*, I think. Ha ha – *amiright? High five.*)

My mum continues. "Sometimes you just have to take it on the chin, and work hard at the opportunities you *do* have. We just have to do better for our kids."

Then she addresses me. "Are you listening to this, too, Jessica? You can be anything you want to be. You can be a forensic scientist if you like. Don't let Mrs Grimshaw or anyone put you off, if that's what you want to be."

"Who's Mrs Grimshaw?" I ask.

"My school careers advisor," replies my mum.

"Oh," I say. Then, "I think I want to be a cartoonist or an artist."

My mum purses her lips, as if she is trying not to react in an annoyed way. "Well, I think you might do better to think about being a forensic scientist."

"No, Jessica, seize the day," interrupts my dad. "If you want to be an artist, move heaven and earth to become an artist. Life is short and it goes by very quickly. Before you know it, you're my age with three kids to support."

Hmmm. I am not exactly convinced that this is an example of *excellent parenting*. It's not really my fault my parents chose to burden themselves by procreating. On the other hand, I *like* that my dad wants me to become an artist.

"Look, just focus on what you *can* do, Bert," says my mum. "The energy-saving light bulbs are brilliant. We love them, *don't we, Jessica*?"

"Yes," I say quickly, getting Mum's vibe. "And the bird feeder has definitely attracted more birds to the garden."

My dad brightens. "It *has,* hasn't it?"

He beams, then falters. "But I just feel like I could be doing more to help the planet."

"Well, one step at a time," replies my mum.

One step at a time is surprisingly good advice from my mum. Normally she wants everything done yesterday. Especially my homework that was due in yesterday. (Ha ha, I am unstoppable.)

"Ryan! Dinner!"

So what has two thumbs, *Super Saver Value* macaroni cheese for dinner and two crazy parents obsessed with missed opportunities? *This guy!* I am pointing at myself with my thumbs but you knew that, right?

Chapter 3

"You can do it, Nat. *Eye of the tiger*," I whisper. Amelia frowns at me like I'm weird.

"Eye of the tiger," Nat repeats quietly to herself. Amelia doesn't comment.

"You'll be brilliant. We practised all lunch, you definitely know it," I add.

"Yeah," whispers Nat.

It's school-musical audition day. Tension is in the air. For Year Six at Hillfern Juniors, the morning lessons seemed like an inconvenience to be got through as fast as possible before auditions could take place this afternoon.

Well, not for me. We have double Art on Tuesday mornings, which I *love*. Also I hate acting and I'm not interested in being in the musical. *But*, I've been told I can be quite heavily involved in *set design* which I *am* excited about.

Plus, while we're all sitting here cross-legged in the Hall, we're *not* in double science. (Although actually I don't really mind science.)

"Yeah, I definitely know it." Natalie repeats my words, sounding as though she's trying to convince herself.

Nat really has her eyes on the prize. She's after the role of Dorothy, the lead. I've not seen her this determined since she believed a rumour that the American pop star, Megan Flyer, was going to open the new shoe shop in our local mall and made us get there at eight o'clock on a Saturday morning, and then made us wait all day for no reason. Still (as my Auntie Joan would say) it's a *story*. Just not a very good one.

Our school musical this year is *The Wizard of Oz*, and our teachers have cunningly worked out that girls are a lot more interested in drama at our age than boys, so they've reworked loads of the parts originally written for boys as "unisex" and a lot of my friends are going for them. I hope they get them.

"I *definitely* know it." Nat repeats my words again, kind of like she's in a trance. I think I'm obviously pretty great at encouragement.

"*I definitely know it,*" Nat says again, in a slightly creepy whisper.

Hmmm. Is this a normal part of audition nerves? I exchange a look of slight concern with Amelia, who clearly thinks it's my fault that Nat has become a broken record or – as my generation should probably call it – a skipping iPod. *Hmm.* That's pretty good. Maybe I should patent that? *Skipping iPod ™ Jessica Morris 2014.*

"Yes, yes, you know it, already." Amelia frowns.

"I *definitely* know it," Nat does that sinister whisper again.

Amelia shoots me another *this-is-on-you-I-hope-you're-happy* evil, which is really quite an impressive sentiment to get across in just one look.

Part of me still sees Amelia as the mean, snooty bully who joined our school at the start of Year 6 and took my best friend away (temporarily) while spreading vicious rumours about my lack of coolness around school. (I mean to be fair, I *am* not cool. But no one really minded until Amelia pointed it out.)

"Maybe you should try and think about something else, something calming," whispers Amelia gently to Nat. Sometimes I wonder why I still see Amelia as that mean girl.

"What you need is a distraction," she continues. "Like ... like, Jessica's hair. Why is it all over to one side like that? Do you think she slept on it funny or did she mean it to be that way? It's been distracting *me* all morning, anyway."

Then I remember. *That's* why. That right there. I still see Amelia as that girl because, well, she *is* still that girl, and she *did* do those things. And it's totally in her to do them again, I reckon. Also, she is a self-proclaimed *daftie*.

But I am supposed to be forgiving and forgetting, and being the bigger person now. And I am. Mainly. In fact, I am *Robert Wadlow* when it comes to Amelia. (He was the tallest man in the world, fact fans.)

"Natalie Baker!" calls Mrs Cole.

Natalie jumps.

"Break a leg!" I whisper-shout as Nat scrambles to her feet and heads over to the stage.

"I thought she was your friend?" whispers Tanya.

Part of me still can't quite believe that *Tanya Harris* is *my* friend now. Sometimes I feel it's like I know the Incredible Hulk in real life, and it turns out he's really good at business stuff and helping to run a secret comic that's cheeky about the school.

"It means good luck," I explain. "Actor people think it's bad luck to say good luck, so they say other stuff instead." I grin. "Nuts, right?"

"OI! Break a leg, Nat!" Tanya suddenly **BReak a LEG!** shouts, making me jump. "Oi! Joshua! Break a leg, innit! Hey Shantair—"

"*Quiet, please!*" Mrs Cole cuts short Tanya's scattergun pep talk.

"It means good luck, Miss," says Tanya happily, seemingly pleased with this new piece of information.

"Yes, well, save your lungs for your own audition, please."

"Sorry, Miss. As you were." Tanya waves amicably

at Mrs Cole as if she's giving her permission to continue.

"OK, then. When you're ready." Mrs Cole addresses Mrs Miller, the music teacher, who starts playing the intro bars on the piano.

My heart is in my throat as Natalie starts singing "Somewhere Over the Rainbow". I feel nervous for her and I really don't want her to mess up, but I needn't have worried – she's *really* good! I always knew she had an amazing voice, but it sounds fantastic all amplified in the big hall like this.

Seriously. I'm not just saying that because we've been best friends since we first heard tell that the enterprising Black Sheep was doing a roaring trade selling wool to his key demographics of master, dame and the little boy who lived down the lane. (I wonder whatever happened to him? I hope the advent of online shopping didn't destroy his business model.)

Natalie is a real natural. And she can dance, too. She's like the full package. We all erupt into applause when she finishes. "That was amazing!" I whisper to her gleefully as she sits back down. "You can't *not* be Dorothy."

"Thanks!" She squeezes my hand, grinning. "And

thanks for believing in me, babes." (*Babes?*) "You saw something in me right from the start and I'm truly blessed to have you in my life." (*Blessed?*)

Since when did Natalie talk like that? There's something vaguely unsettling in the way that it sounded like half an Oscar acceptance speech. I really hope this isn't a sign that Natalie is going to become one of those Crazy Actress types. I'm sure it's not and she's just excited. Yeah, that'll be it.

The rest of the auditions pass by quite uneventfully. Everyone is pretty much as good or bad as I would have expected them to be. The only real surprise is Joshua.

Joshua is auditioning for the part of the Scarecrow and so he sings, "If I Only Had a Brain". But not only that. He (a) sings it really well – I had no *idea* he could sing; and (b) he does this sort of comedy dance to it as well, where he keeps nearly falling over. He gets some really good laughs throughout his performance.

"Wow, Joshua is *brilliant*," Nat whispers to me,

when he's finished.

"I *know*!" I whisper back, shocked.

"He's certainly gone up in my estimation," whispers Amelia, grudgingly. Typical of Amelia to be snide about it.

She's still annoyed because she thinks it's cool to be friends with boys (especially "cool" boys from the basketball team). But hanging out with Joshua didn't exactly lead to the *access-all-areas* cool-boy-party I think Amelia had hoped it might. Instead it led to Lewis making us watch the original Star Wars films from  the 70s and 80s. *I* at least enjoyed them.

"So, *so* good," whispers Nat, still in awe.

I had no idea Joshua was so talented at slapstick. Or the whole performing arena, in fact. How could I not *know* this about him? I mean, I know he has a good sense of humour because we make each other laugh all the time, but *still*.

All the way home, I keep thinking about it. I'm only half listening to my parents over dinner talking about their new shopping budget and trying to negotiate with Ryan the merits of Tracker Bars over Wagon Wheels. (KitKats are non-negotiable.)

And later still, when I'm playing pirate Lego with Ryan and Lady (Ryan pretty much insists she's everywhere he is) I can't shake off this feeling that I don't know Joshua as well as I thought I did.

Part of me wants to text or call him and say congrats, but I feel weirdly shy. Like he would have told me about the whole singing-and-dancing thing already if he wanted to.

Ha. I mean, you think you know someone.

Natalie got the part! She's going to be Dorothy. I *knew* she would. I might be psychic. (I even know what you're thinking right now. You're thinking: Jessica is *not* psychic. See? Ha! Of course I'm not psychic. Or *am* I? Um, no. No, I'm not. Or *am* – we could be here all day.)

"Oh my God! Like, totally congratulations," gushes Amelia on Wednesday morning as we crowd around the list of names up on the noticeboard.

"I *knew* you'd get it," I say, excitedly. I don't bother to tell them I might be psychic. I'll give them a chance to *sense* it first.

"Oh my God, I'm the Cowardly Lion!" gasps Shantair delightedly, finding her name on the list.

"Hey, congrats!" I tell her, pleased. Shantair, being one of my chess-club friends, is a bit shy so has been trying to do more drama to overcome it. A lion looking for courage seems like an apt role for her in some ways.

"Joshua is the scarecrow," says Amelia, as we get slightly jostled to the side by other people crowding round the list. (Would it kill my school to stick up more than one list?)

"Budge over," comes a friendly but firm instruction from Tanya Harris, arriving at the chaos.

"Yes! Get in!" she shouts then, GET IN! punching the air and nearly injuring several people. "I'm the Bad Witch! Mwahah haha haha!" She does her witchy cackle, then saunters off singing, "Ding Dong, the Witch is Dead."

Hmmm. Shantair is shy and gets to be the Cowardly Lion, Tanya is … well, Tanya … and gets to be the Bad Witch. I'm not saying my school is typecasting its pupils but – no wait, I am. My school is *totally* typecasting its pupils.

Oh no, wait, Amelia is the *Good* Witch, so that's that theory blown out of the water. Ha ha.

"Is this the *final* list?" I hear an aggrieved and disappointed voice ask. A voice that is not *used* to disappointment.

The crowd starts to disperse and Harriet VanDerk is left staring dejectedly at the noticeboard, scanning and re-scanning it for her name. I almost feel sorry for her. *Almost.*

"It looks like it says here I'm the understudy's understudy," explains Harriet, "and that can't be right, can it?"

Poor Harriet, maybe I do feel a tiny bit sorry for—

"I mean, I'm better than all of *you*," she finishes scornfully.

Nah, scrub that, I don't feel sorry for her at all.

Harriet VanDerk is *very* competitive. Her family live next door to mine and they are also *very* competitive. I think it must get passed on genetically.

The downside for me is that the VanDerks bring out the competitive side in my parents and then my parents wonder why I don't win spelling bees or come top of the class in things that aren't Art. This can be quite a nuisance if you just want to relax and watch TV instead of bettering yourself all the time.

Personally, I think Harriet VanDerk didn't get a better part because her acting was very wooden at the auditions. She's the best at everything that isn't arty because she's so regimented in her approach.

Surely *most* people would be delighted they were best at *nearly* everything, but not Harriet. She can't live and let live, or abide having anyone beat her. She wants world domination and all the prizes for herself.

Obviously it would be rude to tell her this, though. So, like an *EastEnders'* character, I was going to have to *leave it out*. "I think it is the final list, yeah," I say awkwardly.

"Well, we'll just see about that," says Harriet, and storms off down the corridor.

I, on the other hand, am *delighted* to have officially bagged the "part" of set design. I sigh with contentment later in double English, as I think about how much fun it's going to be. I think I'm going to be *awesome* at it. I'm totally an *artist* now.

Last term, when we had to do the wildlife project, I drew a really good (and big) picture of a badger, and the lady that came to judge our work (a real lady, not my new dog) said basically that I am an artist. So don't just take my word for it.

Obviously, it hasn't changed me. Or made me in any way pretentious. Weirdly, if anything, it's calmed me down a bit. (I got a bit obsessed with our comic last term.) But now that I've had what my sister Tammy calls "outside validation" I feel more relaxed about needing to show off. I can't wait to throw myself into the set design and do the best job I can.

I'll be truly creative, hanging around in the background, building and painting things, but I'll still get to hang out with all my friends in the musical. It's almost *too perfect*.

Whoa.

Don't think *that,* Jessica, I warn myself. That's what someone says in a sitcom right before they cut to the comic disaster that upends their plans.

"Yeah, easily," I hear Amelia say to Natalie as the bell goes and we start packing up our books for break time. "I'm really good at stuff like this, and I like getting the extra credit. Plus my part is quite small anyway."

"What extra credit?" I ask, arriving at their desks.

"Amelia is involved in the set design side of things, too," Nat explains happily.

Noooooooooo! And there it is. The comic disaster. I've brought this on myself by thinking like a sitcom. Universe – I take it back, it wasn't *too perfect*. It was just right. *Undo, undo!*

"I'm really good at organising things," Amelia smiles at me. "I'm a naturally bossy person. Plus, you know, I love it!"

Urgh. For God's sake. Being a *naturally bossy person* is nothing to be proud of. And you don't get into set design because you love organising things and bossing people around. Surely the only acceptable reason to get into set design is because you want to *design sets*.

Typical. Still, at least I'm really good at ignoring **TYPICAL**

her sarky swipes these days. I am *Robert Wadlow*,
remember.

I finally get to talk to Joshua properly at the lunchtime
comic meeting. (I mean, I gave him the thumbs up
after his audition and everything, but it's not the
same.)

"Your scarecrow song and dance was amazing!"
I tell him as we sit on the comfy seats outside the
library, also known as the Quiet Reading Area (our
unofficial *Hell*fern comic HQ). "Congrats on getting
the part."

"Ahem," says Tanya. "What about me and all,
Toons?"

"Well, yes, obviously you were brilliant too,
Tanya," I say quickly. "But I knew you … I mean, I
didn't know Joshua … could even hold a tune."

"Charming," says Joshua loftily.

"You know what I mean," I say, feeling awkward.
It's difficult trying to keep everyone's egos happy. Is
this going to be the downside of being surrounded
by actors? Will I be expected to give out loads of
compliments all the time now? "You never said you
could sing," I add.

"Dark horse, inne?" says Tanya. "Like me."

"Tanya, you're always shouting and singing," I point out. "Mostly shouting, to be fair."

"Yeah, but that's just the tip of the iceberg. I got lots going on. Don't box me in, Toons. I'm deep, innit."

I wonder if this would be a good opportunity to do an impression of my friends, like, "Oooh, look at me, I'm an *actor* now. I'm all deep and important." But I decide against it. I don't know if actors have a sense of humour. Anyway, they're probably just excited they've both got their dream parts, and that's why they're taking it all so seriously.

"Congrats to you *both*. I think you're both going to be brilliant in the musical," I say, meaning it.

"Cheers," says Tanya appreciatively.

"Yeah, cheers," says Joshua. "So, let's talk comic. I still really want to collaborate with you on the Parents' Handbook idea."

"Great," I say.

"But I think it might take longer than a couple of

lunchtimes," he adds. "So we should look at some other times we're all free to meet up."

"That don't clash with rehearsals," says Tanya.

"Oh yeah, good point," amends Joshua.

"Well yeah, but there should be plenty of time for both, shouldn't there?" I say.

I mean, I am an *expert* at juggling lots of things. Well, actually maybe *expert* isn't quite the right word. *Disaster* might be more accurate, in fact. But I learned from my past mistakes, so I can *stelp* ™ them from doing the same.

I make the point that if the Year Six Wildlife Project didn't halt production of *Hell*fern last term, then the musical shouldn't this term. The others agree with me, though I think I catch Tanya and Joshua exchange a slight look of concern. Or did I imagine it? Lewis doesn't seem to have noticed anything.

"Well, what about Saturday?" suggests Joshua. "We could meet at the mall and get slushies and do some work on it then."

"You just love that slushie place," I say.

"Who wouldn't?" he replies.

"It's got ice, it's got flavours… What's not to love?" He grins. So we agree to meet at The Slush Pile on Saturday and work on the comic then.

Although I'm worried for their sanity, it's not just the actors who are excited about the musical. I'm really looking forward to designing the set, even if the chief member of DAFT will be there, breathing down my neck.

I'm not a hundred per cent sure what to expect, but Mrs Cooper, our Art teacher, said it might be an idea to start picturing how we think the set should look, and researching online how other productions have done it.

I'm *way* ahead of her. I've done my online research and am just sketching out some rough ideas of things I think look good. (Which is lucky because my dad is *totally hogging* the family laptop now.)

"Daddy, how much longer are you going to be?" asks Ryan, eyeing up the laptop on my dad's knee later that Wednesday evening.

The three of us are sitting in the living room, the news is on quietly in the background, Lady is lying on Ryan's feet and I'm sketching out potential set ideas in preparation for the first rehearsal tomorrow.

"You have to learn to be patient and share, Ryan," replies my dad. "And I *happen* to be reading rather an important article. It says that the Deanbury Forest is under threat from plans to build a new bypass."

"Are you on Horace King's website again?" I ask, looking up. (Is Mum right? Is Dad getting a bit obsessed?)

"Jessica, if they tear down all those trees to build a new road it will have a devastating effect on the local bird population," my dad replies tersely. But I notice he doesn't actually answer my question.

"But Daddy, I want to play on *Cbeebies*," whines Ryan.

I think my dad is about to tell Ryan off for whining,

but then there is a shout from the other room.

"*Wait* till you see what *your dog* has done *now*!"

Even from the next room, I think I can tell that my mum *might* be a *tiny* bit angry.

There's nothing like some quality family time. And this is *nothing* like some quality family time. Ha ha. I've still got it. *Hmmm.*

We each abandon what we're doing and head into the kitchen to see what all the fuss is about.

"Look at this!" My mum is waving  something about. "She's chewed my slippers. Just *my* slippers. None of *your* slippers. Just mine. She's disrespecting me."

"Dogs don't think like that," says my dad.

"Oh yeah?" queries my mum. "I know what she was thinking all right. She's saying *there*, that's what I think of you."

"Maybe you should take it as a compliment?" I suggest. "Maybe your slippers are her *favourites*, and she loves you the best."

"Do you think this is funny?" asks my mum.

"No," I reply, suddenly finding it funny. "If I

thought it was funny I would have made a joke, like, 'Hey, don't put your *foot* in it!' but I didn't."

Ryan chuckles.

"*Jessica*," says my dad warningly.

"Too soon?" I ask.

"How would you like it if she ate *your* slippers?" Mum continues.

"I wouldn't mind," replies Ryan factually. "I hate wearing slippers."

Ah, the quiet wisdom of a six-year-old. My mum is temporarily speechless.

"Well," says dad, trying to gloss over the situation. "Let's just *all* make sure we don't leave things lying around in future."

I wince. Three … two … one…

"*What?*" cries my mum. "Are you saying I run a *messy house*?"

Chapter 5

"OK, is everybody where they need to be?" asks Mrs Cooper at the first after-school rehearsal on Thursday.

Don't worry, we all lived through the shouting match. Well, I say *shouting match*. It was mainly my mum listing everything she does for us; us feeling guilty and promising to do more around the house; and then my dad making her a cup of tea. It's the circle of life. (I'm pretty sure that's what Elton John was singing about in *The Lion King*, anyway.)

"Are you my set designers?" Mrs Cooper addresses a smallish group of pupils. "Gather round, gather round."

Everyone in the class has been feeling quite tense today. Natalie chose sausage and mash for lunch, but then could hardly eat any of it, so I got one of her whole sausages *for free*. Obviously I feel bad that she's so nervous but still, *free sausage*!

"Gather round, gather round!" I hear Mrs Cole shout the same thing from the stage area to the actors. "Stop messing about at the back and come over here."

"Ignore them," Mrs Cooper instructs us set designers. Some music suddenly blares out and then stops. *Hmmm.* I think this ignoring idea might be a *smidge* optimistic. Like trying to ignore Ryan on Bat Day. (Which is every day. Every day is Bat Day for Ryan. Unless my mum confiscates his bat.)

I look around at the other set designers. Apart from Amelia, I like all of them. My friends Emily, Megan and Fatimah are here – this is going to be fun! Harriet VanDerk is here, too, but I think she's about to get sent away to the stage.

"Now then," says Mrs Cooper. "We don't have a lot of time and we have quite a big job, but I know you're all going to work together brilliantly." (We nod.) "OK, great. So, Jessica is our main set designer."

Am I? *Cool!* I'm a *main* set designer! I'm pretty sure I can put this on my CV and then quit school and get a job at an actual theatre! Well, I probably should *design* the set first. Also my mum might kill me.

"Where are my Munchkins? Over here, please!" I hear Mrs Cole shout from the stage. Our heads swivel that way and then back to Mrs Cooper.

"Oh, I sketched out some of the ideas we discussed," I say.

"Excellent," says Mrs Cooper. "You can show me those in a moment."

"Ahem." Harriet coughs loudly, in a sort of fake-cough type way.

"Need a cough sweet?" asks Amelia snidely. Amelia doesn't like Harriet VanDerk any more than I do. I think it's because Harriet normally comes top of the class and Amelia tends to come second.

"What are you doing here, Harriet?" asks Emily. "I thought you were an understudy."

"To an understudy." Amelia obviously can't help herself.

"No, that was a mistake," replies Harriet. (I don't like the way this is going.)

48

"Harriet … felt like she'd have more to offer here," explains Mrs Cooper kindly.

Nooooooooo! Not Harriet. NOOOOOOO! What is the universe playing at? I've already had my sitcom-style disappointment over *Amelia* being here. I don't need *two* people ruining one of the funnest things that's ever happened to me. One is plenty. *Plenty*.

"Yes," asserts Harriet. "We discussed it, and everyone thought my many skills would be perfect to head up the set-design team."

"Well, not," says Mrs Cooper, "that's not quite…" She stops herself. I think she was going to say that's not quite *true*, but she obviously doesn't want to hurt Harriet's feelings in front of everyone. "More about teamwork, wasn't it? Anyway, let's get on, lots to get through."

Huh, I think. Translation: After failing to secure a part in the musical itself – due to very wooden acting – Harriet has gone and complained about it, in the grand tradition of spoilt people used to always getting their own way. Then she's been given an ego-saving, nonsense role as something vague which she is already trying to pretend means she's in charge of us.

This is pretty much *nightmare scenario one* for me, and we haven't even been here five minutes.

"Let's see then, Jessica," says Mrs Cooper, as Munchkins leap-frog over each other in the background. I show her the drawing I have done of the yellow brick road.

I thought it could be one of the main backdrops, so it starts off with the road really wide at the bottom of the picture, then gets thinner and thinner as it goes away, over the hills.

It will look like the cast can really walk down it – but actually if they tried they'd just be walking into a flat wall.

"I love this, Jessica," states Mrs Cooper, sounding gratifyingly impressed.

"I suppose it's not *too* bad," says Harriet, peering over my shoulder. "*I* would have done it differently."

"Harriet, would you like to go and start counting up the paintbrushes?" asks Mrs Cooper quickly. I wonder briefly if she's just trying to get Harriet out of our hair by giving her *busywork*.

This thought may be crossing Harriet's mind too, as she frowns but heads over to where all the equipment has been laid out.

"Great," says Mrs Cooper. "OK, if you draw this up neatly first, you can copy it out carefully on to the canvas, and then everyone can help paint it in. There will be other backdrops to discuss of course, but this is a *great start*. Well done."

"Thanks," I say, beaming. This is so exciting! I'm going to draw my first set design!

As I'm carefully drawing the picture out neatly, Amelia and Harriet arrive at the table next to me and start measuring out some of the canvas.

"I wonder who will be in charge of getting the ruby slippers?" muses Harriet.

"Wardrobe, probably," replies Amelia, sounding uninterested.

"Well, they're pretty important," continues Harriet (either not detecting or not caring that Amelia would rather not be sucked into a conversation with her). "They're kind of like the Chekhov's gun," she adds grandly. The *what now*?

"Fascinating," replies Amelia dryly, sounding anything but fascinated.

"What's a Chekhov's gun?" I can't help but ask. My curiosity gets the better of me every time.

Amelia looks annoyed that I have asked this, as it clearly gives Harriet exactly what she wants – the chance to show off.

Harriet (predictably enough) rolls her eyes at my ignorance, before deigning to answer. "Oh my God, don't you know?" (That's why I'm asking, I think, patiently.) "Sometimes I forget I'm the only one here who really knows about *proper drama*," she continues.

"Fine, don't tell me. I'll Google it," I reply.

"Oh bless," says Harriet, clearly enjoying herself. "Chekhov is a really famous Russian writer from the Victorian times. 'Chekhov's Gun' is the dramatic principal he wrote his plays by."

"Uh-uh," I say, now definitely regretting asking.

But Harriet isn't done enlightening me. "He thought that everything in a story should be necessary and irreplaceable," she continues. "And anything not necessary should be removed. So basically, putting it into *layman's* terms, if there is a story with a gun in it at the beginning, by the end of the story, the gun should have gone off. Otherwise the gun shouldn't be in the story."

"So you're saying the ruby slippers 'go off' by the end of the *Wizard of Oz*?" I say.

"Exactly." Harriet beams. "See, that wasn't so hard to understand, was it?" she simpers patronisingly.

"Interesting," I say. "But I don't think I agree with Chekhov."

"*What?*" Harriet seems flummoxed. (I see Amelia smirk out of the corner of my eye.) "Why not?" demands Harriet.

"Well, that just sounds like it will be a very predictable story," I explain. "If you *know* for *certain* that *every* gun will go off, there'll be no surprises and that's going to get boring. Surely you need *some* red herrings in there, you know, for jeopardy, to add a bit of *will they, won't they*."

"You can't *disagree* with Chekhov," says Harriet crossly. "You obviously just don't get it."

"I *do* get it," I say indignantly. "You don't have to be so rude to me, Harriet. *Honestly*. And I thought *Amelia* was bad. No offence, Amelia."

"None taken," says Amelia dryly, though she looks somewhat satisfied that Harriet's feathers have been ruffled.

"I'm not being rude," says Harriet. "You're just immature."

"Hah," I joke. "Would an immature person be a

member of a secret gang called DAFT?"

"You say it D.A.F.T.," interrupts Amelia automatically but she looks slightly like she's trying not to laugh. Slightly.

Before Harriet can respond, Mrs Cooper comes over.

"Great work, girls. This is looking good. Lovely." She pauses. "Now then, I'll need two people, perhaps Jessica and Amelia, to have a look at these colour samples." She plops some bits of paper on to the tables. "Decide which one will be the best yellow, so I can order the paint."

Oh, blimey. I'm not the most decisive person in the world. I feel under pressure now. Plus I'm really not sure Amelia and I are the right combo to agree on something.

I glance at Harriet and see she's frowning. This is definitely a job she would have liked to do. And she probably doesn't think I deserve to do it, as I have just disagreed with her good friend Chekhov.

Mrs Cooper saunters away. The people on stage start singing "We're Off to See the Wizard". Amelia looks disdainfully at me. "Well," she says, studying the samples. "Not that one, that one, or that one." She tosses three aside.

"Um, it's meant to be a joint decision," I say.

"Yes," says Harriet. "Maybe I should do it? If you two can't get along like you were asked."

"No, no," replies Amelia quickly, visibly irked. She exhales calmly. "OK, Jessica. I'm *listening*. Which one do *you* think is the best?" She says it kind of slowly and contemptuously.

"Um. Well." I look at the colours. "Not *Lemon Sorbet*, it's too pale. And *Lantern* is kind of greeny." *Hmmm.* "I think something brighter, so that it's visible and a good contrast but doesn't dominate the stage. So … either *Sunny Side Up* or *Banana Time*. I think *Honey* and *Straw* are just a tiny bit too dark and browny. But maybe one could work for the brick definition? *Tropical* is too bright and luminous. Let's go with Banana Time."

"Those are actually … all really good points." Amelia sounds surprised but impressed by my thought process. "OK, then. *Banana Time* it is." She smiles.

Ha! Who knew *that* could happen? And I am totally

better at making decisions than I thought I was.

"I don't like it." Harriet peers disapprovingly at the sample. "I think you've made the wrong choice."

"Well, it doesn't matter what *you* think," replies Amelia, bluntly.

Harriet carries on regardless. "I don't know why Mrs Cooper didn't ask *me* to choose the colours. I'm much better at this type of thing than you are."

"*Whatever*," Amelia sneers. "Don't you have some paintbrushes to count?"

But Harriet is undeterred. "By the way, Amelia," she continues. "You should really have your hair tied back for this kind of work. *It's not a fashion show.*"

Wow. Did Harriet just kind of *slam* Amelia? I have mixed feelings about this.

Amelia looks livid for a second, then she composes herself and replies, "Well, *you* would know."

Pow. Amelia just slammed Harriet right back.

God, I'm so confused. I don't know who to root for. I spend the rest of rehearsal wondering if I should have just offered to high-five both of them.

Chapter 6

You know what's great about being forced to work in close proximity to Harriet VanDerk? That's right. *Nothing.*

On my way home from school the next day (Friday), I find my mum chatting to Mr and Mrs VanDerk over the little hedge in the front garden. This is generally always a bad sign.

Normally one of three things will happen next:

1   My mum will find out about some academic achievement that Harriet has aced and I have bombed at, then be annoyed with me for not trying harder, and *be in a bad mood.*

2   My mum will try to boast about something one of us has done, only to be outdone by a VanDerk,

and *be in a bad mood.*

3   My mum will boast about one of the *very rare* things one of us has actually beaten a VanDerk at, and temporarily be in a *good* mood. Which *looks* like a victory – but it's not. (It's just pressing snooze on failure.) Because later she will wonder why we can't do that *all the time*, and so *be in a bad mood.*

I mean, to be honest, they could just chat about the weather and somehow the VanDerk weather will be better than our weather, and my mum will end up in a bad mood.

Personally, I think the best course of action is avoidance, but that's hard when you live next door, and anyway sometimes the VanDerks lurk and wait for us, their hapless prey.

"Well, I want the new bypass to go ahead," I hear Mrs VanDerk say as I reach them. "It will definitely shave time off my commute. And I mean what's a few trees here and there when I could lie in for another fifteen minutes each day!" She chuckles, and Mr VanDerk joins in.

"Hear, hear," he agrees. "Ah, here's young Jessica, hello there!"

"Hi," I reply.

"Hi, poppet." My mum puts her arm around me and kisses the top of my head. "How was school?"

Before I can answer, Mr VanDerk says, "I hope you've started behaving yourself for our little Harriet. She's head of the set-design team, you know. You have to obey her."

"You … *what*?" I say, fighting a mad urge to laugh.

Blimey. Harriet has actually *lied* to her parents about her role in the musical production. I guess she must be so used to having to tell them impressive things, she's, er, *massaged the figures* a bit.

"Um, I'm not sure what Harriet's told you but that's not quite right," I say tentatively. "Actually *I'm* the main set designer. That's what Mrs Cooper said."

"Yes," says my mum, deciding to join in even though she knows very little about the subject. "Our *Jessica* is the main set designer," she repeats unnecessarily. *Ohh*. I don't want to get sucked into whatever this is.

The VanDerks stare at me, momentarily bamboozled, then Mr VanDerk recovers himself. "Well, you might be the *main* set designer, but Harriet is the *head* set designer. So she still delegates to you. And we don't want you giving her any more trouble."

Honestly. This family are *unbelievable*. They are just insane. Mum and I need to walk away, right now.

"What trouble?" asks my mum. "What are you implying?" *Noooo*. Stop it, Mum!

"Jessica and a girl called Amelia were a bit cheeky to Harriet yesterday about some paint," says Mr VanDerk.

"That really isn't what happened," I say.

"No harm done," says Mr VanDerk, as if I have apologised. "But just think about it in the future."

Possibly because my mum knows I don't really get on with a girl called Amelia, she seems to believe me and doesn't publically pursue this. Everyone says goodbye and goes into their respective houses. But when we are inside, my mum wants to know exactly what's going on. I explain it to her as best I can.

"But then Harriet's *lying*," she concludes correctly. "I'm not having that little madam throwing her weight around as if she owns the place. Or having them next door lording it up over things that aren't even true."

"Mum, it's fine. If anything it's sad that Harriet has lied about this."

"I'm not having your good name besmirched," replies my mum adamantly. *What good name?* I wonder.

"Are you sure you're not just annoyed because it's a VanDerk?" I ask her. "If it was anyone else I'm sure you'd tell me to ignore them and just get on with my job." My mum considers this for a moment.

"I'm hungry!" I hear my sister's voice coming from the next room.

"Tammy!" I run into the kitchen and give her a hug.

"How's the new dog?" asks Tammy.

"Brilliant," I say. "She and Ryan are mainly inseparable."

"The VanDerks are pro the new bypass," comments my mum, getting two frozen supermarket brand pizzas out of the freezer, while my dad chops salad.

(Woohoo! Friday night pizza! Take *that,* economy drive.)

"*Quelle surprise,*" retorts Tammy. "That's so typical of them. *That* alone should be enough to put you off it. You should definitely help provide snacks for the protest now."

"*Protest?*" My dad's ears appear to have pricked up. "There's going to be a protest? To save the forest?"

"Too right there is," says Tammy. "If allowed to happen, this forest-murder will be an *atrocity*." (My dad nods seriously.) "And it's all the result of big money running the world." Tammy is warming to her subject. "This is the trouble with capitalism, you know. *The Man* is destroying the future of the planet for a quick buck."

"Absolutely, absolutely," my dad agrees.

Lady enters the kitchen with something hanging out of her mouth. It takes us a second to realize that it's post.

"Lady, *drop*," commands my dad. Lady drops the chewed-up, saliva-soaked letter on the floor and wags her tail.

"Good dog!" My dad tells her.

"She *isn't* good if she's chewed our post," observes my mum.

Lady wisely takes this as her cue to leave and runs back out of the kitchen. My mum bends to pick up the soggy letter. "This is a bill. It's a real nuisance. Things can't go on like this."

I decide I can't be bothered to listen to my parents and sister debate the merits of dog training, so I head upstairs.

I find Lady and a space-helmeted Ryan in his bedroom, sitting under an improvised tent-spaceship (a blanket tied to his wardrobe-door handle). Ryan appears to have made Lady a makeshift space helmet out of a cardboard box.

"Ryan, I'm not sure that's—"

"All aboard!" says Ryan, when he sees me. "To the moon! We'll be safe there."

I crawl in next to them, unsure whether to point out that with no breathable atmosphere, we'll probably be *less* safe on the moon. But Ryan seems happy to make the engine and booster noises of our journey, while leaning left and right, so I don't bother.

"Hey, Ryan?" I say, after we have disembarked by the Apollo Lunar Model (his stuffed T-Rex).

"Yes?"

"We really love Lady, don't we?"

"Yes." Ryan instantly puts his arm around her.

"And we want her to stay with us, don't we?"

"*Yes*," says Ryan firmly.

"Mum is getting really annoyed with her chewing stuff. I was thinking, how about you and I keep an eye out and move anything out of her reach that we think she might be likely to chew? You know, just keep the place a bit tidier so she can't get in any more trouble?"

"Yes. OK. Definitely," replies Ryan, and we shake on it.

Something vibrates in my pocket and I realise my phone is ringing. "Hang on, Ryan, I have to get this," I say, feeling like an important person in a film.

It's Joshua! "Hello," I say, trying not to sound too happy as I close my bedroom door. "What time shall we meet tomorrow?"

"That's what I'm ringing about," says Joshua. "I'm really sorry but I don't think I can meet you at the mall to plan out The Parents' Handbook. And I don't think Tanya can, either. We were talking about it, and we think maybe we should be trying to learn our lines instead."

"Oh, OK," I say. Blimmin' actors, I think. *Already* so flakey, what a stereotype!

"You're not annoyed, are you?" he asks.

"Well. No," I say reasonably. I mean, if you're happy to be a stereotype, then so be it! I don't add that, though. "I'm pretty much the coolest person in the world, so of course not," I say.

He chuckles. "Yeah. That's what everyone says about you."

"It is? I *knew* it!" I joke. He laughs.

Oh well, I guess these things can't be helped. And I'm sure when they feel a bit more confident in their roles it will all calm down again. We chat for a bit and then hang up when Joshua's dinner is ready.

Hmm. Now I have a free Saturday. I know, I'll call Nat and see if she wants to go swimming with me instead. That'll be fun.

But when I get through to Nat she tells me she's too busy learning her lines to come out.

"Thanks *loads* for thinking of me, though," she gushes down the phone.

Well, of course I *thought* of you, I think, bemused. You're my best friend. It's a shame she can't squeeze me in for even *half an hour*, though. We always *used* to make time for each other, no matter what was happening. *Hmmm*, I think, remembering the wildlife project and all that went wrong there... Still, though, I did *try*.

OK, then. Another pirate-Lego marathon with Ryan it is. I wonder what percentage of the time he will wear his space helmet?

Chapter 7

Sixty per cent, fact fans. I roughly calculate my brother kept his space helmet on for about sixty per cent of the weekend. (He was forced to take it off for meals and when my dad took us swimming and to the library.)

A weekend of line-learning doesn't seem to have chilled everyone out much, I observe on Monday morning. Natalie seems jittery, Joshua is unusually quiet, and even Tanya appears to have bags under her eyes.

Every chance I get during break and lunch I tell Natalie that she's going to be brilliant, but it doesn't seem to cheer her up much. (Though I do score some of the chips at lunch that she can't finish again. *Obviously* I'd still much rather she didn't feel so nervous, but, you know, every cloud.)

"Oh God, why do I do this to myself?" says Natalie dramatically, as the end-of-school bell goes and we start heading to the after-school rehearsal.

"Because you're a *star*, daaahling!" I reply in a funny voice.

Nat laughs and hugs me. "God, what would I do without you, Jess?" she says.

"See you on the other side," I reply. "I've got to go draw stuff while Harriet VanDerk complains." Nat laughs again. Well, at least I seem to have finally cheered her up a little bit.

"Hi," says Amelia, as I join her in the hall. The giant piece of canvas that I sketched the yellow brick road on to has been spread out over several tables that have been put together and now we have the fun task of painting it in.

"Hi," I reply. As ever, I'm feeling slightly tense around Amelia, like I might be insulted at any moment.

"I wonder what Her Majesty, Queen Of The World will accuse us of today," she says dryly.

Her comment catches me off guard and I chuckle. "Ha, yeah," I reply.

"The paint's arrived," she adds, lifting a big pot of *Banana Time* on to a chair next to the tables.

I never realised that Amelia has quite a funny sarcastic side. (Maybe because it's normally directed at me?) Does this mean we really are *actually* moving towards that elusive territory known as *friendship* now?

"It's quite hard to open." Amelia gestures to the lid. "And I have nice nails, so as yours are already really ugly, maybe you could open it?"

Yeah, maybe *not*. Frenemies it is. At least I know where I stand. Using the end of a paintbrush, I manage to get the pot open and we start painting.

Over on the stage, we can hear the rehearsal going on.

"Oh, Aunty Em! Aunty Em!" cries Natalie, holding a stuffed toy dog. That's Toto.

Hannah (who likes my cartoons – I drew a rabbit for her once) is Aunty Em and replies, "Not now, Dorothy!"

"But Aunty Em, that mean Miss Gulch hit Toto! Just because he chased her nasty old cat!"

Mrs Cooper is floating around issuing instructions and drawing some things herself. Fatimah and Megan are sent to help us. (They've been separated from Emily – unfairly, they reckon – for talking more than working.)

"I'll get you! And your little dog, too!" shouts Tanya from the stage, before cackling madly. I have to say, I *love* Tanya as the bad witch. She does being evil so joyfully.

"Oh, hello there." Harriet approaches our table.

She smiles sweetly. "You're using the wrong paint, by the way."

Amelia and I exchange a look. "No, we're not," says Amelia.

"We're just using a colour you don't like," I add.

"Don't assume, it makes an ass of u and me," replies Harriet smugly.

"No, it doesn't," I say.

"What?" Harriet pauses. "Not *another* thing you don't get, Jessica?" She smirks. "I know you're not great at spelling so let me help you. You spell assume a-s-s—"

"No, I get what you've done, but it doesn't work," I reply.

"It does work, it's an aphorism," explains Harriet tiredly.

I'm getting a bit irritated by Harriet's superior attitude now.

"It doesn't work, actually. Because it doesn't turn 'u' and 'me' into an 'ass', it just puts an 'ass' next to 'u' and 'me'."

"Kind of like what's happening now," comments Amelia. I splutter laughter in spite of myself.

"Fine, be like that, I'm just trying to help," replies

Harriet loftily and saunters off again.

Phew, I think. The four of us relax and Megan introduces the old "Would You Rather?" game from back in Art lessons. Amelia has never played it before.

"Really?" Fatimah sounds shocked.

"What have you been doing with your life?" I joke.

Amelia looks for a moment like she wants to say something cutting, but then maybe realises that with us three as her audience, there is no one "cool" to impress, so decides to just roll with it. "How do you play?" she asks.

For the next half hour, we chat and have fun while we're painting, and I learn various useless facts about Amelia.

For example, she would rather have pencils than cooked sausages for fingers; and she would rather have to end every sentence with the word "wibble" than the word "munchkin".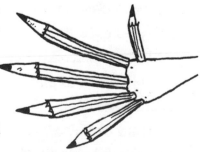

"OK," says Megan. "I've got one.

Which would you rather give up *for ever*: chocolate or cheese?"

"Are you allowed to still eat goat's cheese?" asks Amelia. We consider this.

"No," responds Fatimah.

"Then I would give up chocolate," says Amelia.

"*What?*" I cry. "No chocolate!"

"I'm playing the odds," says Amelia. "Cheese is in everything. I still get to eat pizza, carbonara sauce..."

"She's right," says Megan.

"I *would* miss pizza," I concede. "But I couldn't live without chocolate." (Yikes, do I sound like Ryan?)

We've filled in nearly three quarters of the yellow brick road when Harriet and Mrs Cooper come over.

"You see, Mrs Cooper?" says Harriet. "They've used the wrong paint." (What is she up to *now*?)

"We haven't," I assert. "We've used *Banana Time* just like you wanted us to."

"Oh, no!" says Mrs Cooper. "That *is* the wrong paint, girls." She puts her hands round her neck in a pose of mild anguish.

"But it's the one we chose and you said you were going to order it," says Amelia.

"Well, yes, but then it got changed," explains Mrs Cooper. "Harriet spotted that *Trumpet* was on special offer, so I changed the order to that. *Banana Time* is just for shading in the pathway so it looks like bricks. Harriet, didn't you tell them this was the wrong paint?"

"Yes," says Harriet smugly.

"*No*," say Amelia and I together.

"Well," I amend. "She only *just* told us." And she made it sound like a lie.

"Oh dear, what a terrible mix up," says Mrs Cooper. "I'm awfully sorry, girls, but you're going to have to start again. There isn't going to be enough paint otherwise. Oh dear, oh dear."

"Are you *serious*?" I blurt out. I can't quite believe

this is happening. Or how smug
Harriet looks about the whole
thing.

"Yes." Mrs Cooper looks
nearly as upset as I feel.
"You'll have to leave this
to dry before you can do
anything really. Maybe you
could start on the Poppy Fields
backdrop? But use the *Trumpet*

paint this time… Though actually, there might not be
time now. *Hmmm.* Oh *dear*, I *do* hope we don't get
too behind schedule. What to do?" Mrs Cooper runs
a hand through her hair as she's thinking.

"Well, hopefully now you'll *listen* to me in future."
Harriet turns to us pompously.

"Are you for *real*, Harriet?" I snap.

"How were we supposed to know we could believe
you?" asks Amelia. "All you did at the last rehearsal
was criticise and hassle us. Like some kind of weird
control freak."

Harriet smiles serenely. "Mrs Cooper? Shouldn't
Amelia's hair be tied back for this kind of work?"
POW! (Oh no, she *didn't*!)

Mrs Cooper is snapped out of her reverie. "What? Oh yes, do tie your hair back please, Amelia," she replies absently.

Amelia looks like she might explode but says nothing. I'm pretty sure Harriet has just crossed a line that she may live to regret.

"I'm going to pop back to the office to see if there're any smaller jobs you can get on with for the rest of today," Mrs Cooper says finally. "What a terrible waste of paint and time," she mutters to herself as she walks off.

Harriet folds her arms and smiles at us, satisfied. "I think I've made my point," she says.

"Is your point that you're a massive cow?" asks Megan. All four of us are shooting daggers at Harriet with our eyes, but unfortunately she seems to enjoy it.

"Don't call her that, she'll only tell on you," says Fatimah. "We should just ignore her."

"Ignore me at your peril," retorts Harriet. (*Peril?* Where is she getting this stuff from?) "I'm in charge of set design and you have to do what I say from now on."

Urrgghhh. Desire to kill rising … stay calm, stay calm… I mean, if ever anything was the *living end*, this is it. I think my blood might be boiling. I  wonder if I'm going red. But not from embarrassment, from anger. And I've had *enough*.

"No, you're not, Harriet." I manage to keep my voice even. "You went behind our backs to change the paint colour, and you let us paint most of this picture before you properly intervened. Your behaviour is actually *sabotaging* the whole musical."

"Yeah," agrees Megan.

"It's supposed to be about teamwork," adds Fatimah.

"And there's no 'I' in team," adds Amelia, using one of Harriet's beloved aphorisms against her.

"No, but there is a '*me*' in team," says Harriet smugly. It's highly annoying and we're all momentarily speechless, which gives her the perfect moment to flounce off before I can point out she's got it wrong AGAIN. There isn't a "me" in "team". There's an "m" and an "e" but they are the wrong way round. *Urrrgggghhh.*

"Can you *believe* it?" I ask Nat, still incensed, on the bus home with her and Amelia. I've just relayed the whole story and made myself angry all over again.

"Yeah, that's quite bad," says Natalie, sounding a bit distracted.

"*Quite* bad? *Quite* bad? It's humongously outrageously catastrophic!" I argue.

"Well, now I think you're exaggerating," says Nat calmly.

"Well, I'm not," I say.

"Have you still got time to get all the work done on the set design?" asks Nat.

"Yes, *probably*," I reply. "But it's the principle—"

"Then it's fine," interrupts Nat. "Focus on the positives. That's not a *real* problem. Think about *me*. I'm carrying the whole production!" She laughs, as if she's not outrageously arrogant, but both Amelia and I look at her curiously for a moment.

"Are you?" I query. "I mean, it always struck me as quite a *group* ensemble."

"Yes, I am!" Natalie looks jokily outraged. "I'm the *lead*, Jess. Think about it. All eyes will be on *me*. I'm under a lot of pressure already. You guys should be nice to me and try and lower my stress levels, not add to them with boring stories about Harriet VanDerk." She chuckles again, as if to soften the blow of what she's saying, but Amelia and I don't join in.

BORING

"Well, don't worry," I say. "You're really good, you can do it."

"Thanks, babes," smiles Nat. *Babes?* Seriously, *why* has that come back?

BABES??

The bus pulls in at my stop and we say our goodbyes.

"And for what it's worth," pipes up Amelia, unexpectedly. "I thought it was good when you put Harriet in her place earlier."

"Thanks," I reply, surprisingly pleased by this rare

compliment from my ex-nemesis. Frenemy-nemesis. *Fremenies?* (™ Jessica Morris 2014.) "Shame she didn't listen."

Amelia smiles sadly and I get off the bus feeling confused but, weirdly, slightly more cheerful.

Chapter 8

"OK, Lewis," I say, getting out my pen on Tuesday lunchtime. "Hit me." Lewis looks alarmed. "Not literally," I add. "Just tell me your ideas."

Joshua and Tanya have cancelled an *official lunchtime* comic meeting. This is new, worrying territory. Well, I say *cancelled*, the meeting is going ahead, but they have *absenteed* themselves so they can learn their lines. (*Actors.*)

I'm definitely going to have to have a word with them about this if it continues. It's not fair on Lewis and me. It's especially not fair on me because I'm *dying* to start proper work on the Parents' Handbook idea, but Joshua is still *insisting* I hold off and do it with him.

Talk about having your cake and eating it. He actually had the *audacity* to attempt to *ban* us from talking about it without him. This is definitely the last straw. He is out of chances now. I don't care *how* good he is at funny dancing.

We can't fall behind with our (admittedly self-imposed) schedule. That's what they all told me last term when I was getting upset that they wanted to use this girl Scarlett's cartoons: that I wasn't bigger than the comic. So why should they be? *Hypocrites*.

I mean, I've already had upwards of two people asking when the next issue will be out. (Granted that was Megan and Fatimah at yesterday's after-school rehearsal, before we painted the yellow brick road the wrong colour; I'd casually said, "Blimey, I can't wait for the next issue of *Hell*fern to come out, it's going to be a good one." And they said, "Oh yeah, when will that be?" But it still counts.)

"OK," says Lewis, looking shy but determined.

Lewis is the person I know least out of everyone

on the comic. I quite like him, though. I think. Mainly. We have disagreed in the past because he didn't want Tanya to join the comic, but I did. And he's very serious whereas I'm often joking around, so we sometimes sort of ... *miss* each other.

He's kind of nerdy, and the only person I've ever met who is scared of their own shadow but in a borderline arrogant way.

"OK," he says again, psyching himself up. "So I have this idea: we draw the teachers, but as Star Wars characters."

"Oh, yes?" I say. Lewis is a *huge* Star Wars fan (original films only).

"Great," I say, jotting down some of what he's saying. "That's one idea. Let's come back to that. What else?"

"OK," says Lewis. "So you know how our school musical is the *Wizard Of Oz*?"

"Yes," I nod, getting ready to write. It's weird being the *writer*; Tanya usually does this.

"Well, how about we do a cartoon of all the people in it, but as Star Wars characters?"

"*Um.*" I'm sensing a bit of a theme here. I write this down anyway. "Won't that be confusing?"

"No, like, you know, Dorothy is Princess Leia."

Hmmm.

"Uh, yeah, OK." I pause, trying to be tactful. "What about the Roland comic strip? Have you got any more?" Joshua and Lewis write this really funny comic strip about Roland the Slightly Rubbish Superhero.

"Joshua doesn't want me to do any without him." (*Of course* he doesn't.)

"No, right, OK." I supress a sigh. "Well, maybe you and I could come up with a new comic character?" I suggest brightly, not adding, "Even though we have never worked together on anything before."

"Um…" Lewis looks non-plussed and unenthusiastic. "OK…" He thinks for a moment. "How about a comic all about what Han Solo was thinking while he was in carbonite?"

"From Star Wars?" I confirm.

"Yes." Lewis nods.

"OK, I'm going to write that down, but maybe let's just put a pin in it for now," I say.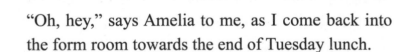

As I told my mum, there's no judgment in blue sky, so it would be wrong to criticise anything Lewis is suggesting. But *still*. I have concerns this issue could end up a bit samey if we're not careful here. Joshua never mentioned that most of his collaboration with Lewis was taken up with *blocking* the Star Wars ideas.

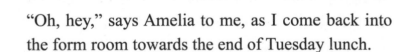

"Oh, hey," says Amelia to me, as I come back into the form room towards the end of Tuesday lunch.

"Hey," I reply, still finding it weirdly unnerving when Amelia is nice to me.

"Oh my God, can one of you hold this hair scrunchie?" Natalie plonks a hairband into Amelia's hand as I join them at their desks.

"What's up?" I ask.

"I'm, like, totally trying to put my hair into pigtails to get into character, but it's really hard without a mirror," replies Natalie, pulling out a plait from one side of her head and starting again.

I suddenly realise I was actually asking Amelia,

not Natalie. That's weird. I suppose it was just the surprise of her addressing me, I thought something must be *up*.

"And what's up with you?" I say to Amelia.

"We've *got* to find a way to deal with Harriet and stop her ruining everything," says Amelia.

"Agreed," I say. "But what?"

"Is this straight?" interrupts Natalie. Before either of us has a chance to reply she says, "It's not, is it? Blimmin' thing." And pulls the plait out again to start over.

"Well," says Amelia. "My mum says when life hands you lemons you have to make lemonade."

"Yeah," I pause. "Well, we probably can't kill Harriet and make her blood into a refreshing soft drink."

To my surprise, Amelia bursts out laughing. I'm genuinely shocked. Normally when I make a joke like that she tells me to stop being gross or something. I don't think I've ever made her laugh before. Intentionally.

"Guys, not helping," comments Natalie crossly.

"Do you want me to do it?" I ask.

"Finally," says Nat. "Thank you. You have to support me, you know. I'm under a lot of pressure with this musical. And now we need to think of a big finish. No one really likes the boring song they want us to end with. We need an all-singing, all-dancing finale."

As I plait Natalie's hair I think for the first time that if the musical really is this much pressure, then maybe she shouldn't be doing it.

On the plus side, we now have supermarket-brand crisps at home, *and* my mum bought us *Mint Aeros*. So I guess life is meant to contain a bit of *ying and yang*.

I can't think of anything to stelp ™ Harriet from being a nightmare, though. And a round of Lego pirates with Ryan just makes me think *walk the plank*, which is probably not an option due to our lack of plank-walking equipment, and the general illegal nature of what really amounts to attempted murder.

Chapter 9

"OK!" booms Mrs Cooper at Thursday's after-school rehearsal.

It's difficult to hear her over the din of the cast learning a dance to "If I Only Had a Brain". The teachers want to incorporate some of Joshua's moves! I'm delighted for him but really think he doesn't need anything else to make him big-headed or distract him from the comic at the moment.

"So get the canvases you were working on last time and put them on to the tables. It's probably a two-person job!" continues Mrs Cooper.

Amelia and I carefully carry our canvas to our tables. "Chop, chop," smiles Harriet as we move past her. And I *just about* manage not to give her the satisfaction of reacting.

Harriet isn't doing anything, I note. Everyone else is helping move tables, or arrange the canvas. But Harriet is just standing around, pretending to be Mrs Cooper's henchman.

"You're right," I say to Amelia, once we are out of earshot. "She's going to drive me mad. We do need to do something."

"I *know*," says Amelia. "And now my hair has this really annoying kink in it from being tied up all the time. I can't get it out. My hair's not coarse like yours, it's really soft, it absorbs each position it's put in."

"Yeah, thanks," I say. "Also that paint stunt that set us back a day and got us into trouble was pretty annoying, too."

Amelia has the good grace to laugh at how self-obsessed she just sounded. "Yes, that too." She smirks. "But I *am* really upset about my hair. Now it's *personal*."

I laugh. *Excellent*. Now it sounds like we're in a film. "It is," I say.

"I'll get you! And your little dog, too!" shouts Tanya from the stage.

"Shhh, Tanya! You're not even in this bit!" chastises Mrs Cole. At least *someone's* enjoying the musical, I think.

"Harriet," I hear Mrs Cooper say. "You don't appear to be doing anything."

Ha! *Justice*. You will have to pull your weight like the rest of us *now*, Harriet VanDerk, I think. Can't dodge it for ever. Amelia and I exchange a satisfied smile.

"Why don't you join Amelia and Jessica and help with the painting?" suggests Mrs Cooper.

Noooooo! Our smiles turn to horrified grimaces. *Ohhh. Don't come over here with your evilness.*

"See how the mighty have fallen," comments Amelia, as Harriet joins us and takes a paintbrush.

"I love your hair like that," replies Harriet unctuously.

I'm still loving them *slamming* each other. Though I'm probably rooting slightly more for Amelia now, even if she did really insult my hair a moment ago.

We paint in tense, miserable silence for bit. Then I have an idea of how to get Harriet back, or at least annoy her momentarily. It's petty and silly. I saw it in a comedy film.

I mumble the word, "Idiot," then say more audibly, "Says what?"

"What?" says Harriet.

"Ha ha!" I laugh. Amelia catches my eye and chuckles.

"What?" Harriet looks at each of us, confused, making us laugh more.

"I said, 'Idiot says what?' And you said, 'What?' You're an idiot," I explain, still chuckling. Harriet looks mystified and annoyed. *Good.*

"Don't tell me you don't *get it*, Harriet?" says Amelia. "Do you want us to explain it again?"

"Oi, Toons!" shouts Tanya from the side of the stage. "Oi! I'm talent now, innit, get us a packet of crisps, ha ha!"

"*Ha!*" I shout back. She'll be lucky. "Let me think about it!" I yell sarcastically. "Oh wait – *NO!*"

"Ha ha!" roars Tanya, turning to Harriet and Amelia. "Oi, Swot-Face! Lady Muck! Get us some crisps!"

"Tanya, get back to what you are supposed to be doing this instant," shouts Mrs Cole.

"It's boring, I'm not in this bit," I hear Tanya say slightly more quietly. I don't catch what Mrs Cole says back.

There's another short silence as Mrs Cole instructs the dancers, and the three of us resume our painting, then Amelia cautiously asks me, "Why does Tanya never bully *you*?"

"Oh, well, that's obvious, isn't it?" Harriet decides to answer on my behalf. "It's because Jessica isn't a *threat* to anyone. She's styled herself as a lovable idiot. Whereas *we're* really clever, so the likes of Tanya Harris are jealous of us. But Jessica has nothing they want."

What? Hang *on*. Just hang on a minute here. What? *Styled* myself – I *am* a lovable idiot. Well, I'm lovable.

"No, it's not that, you clueless moron!" I blurt out. "It's because you're both so bloody smug and rude about how clever you think you are! You put people's backs up. *You're* the *real* bullies who make people feel terrible about themselves. That makes some people lash out. Not everyone can be good at everything. You could both be a lot nicer about it."

They both stare at me for moment. I feel like

I'm panting, even though I'm not. Finally Harriet says, "Well, you keep telling yourself that." But Amelia looks thoughtful, like she has absorbed this information.

"You keep telling yourself it's *jealousy*, then," I retort.

"Face it," says Harriet. "You are just really stupid, Jessica."

"No no no! From the top!" shouts Mrs Cole from the stage. "OK, five, six, seven, eight!" The music starts up.

Urrggghhh. I can't even be bothered to respond. This rehearsal couldn't be more different from the other day when we were painting with Megan and Fatimah and it was *fun*. I glance round the room at my friends, and see they're laughing with Emily. Probably playing the "Would You Rather?" game and having a whale of a time. *Lucky things*. Harriet is like a *fun vacuum*.

"Hi, there," says Mrs Cooper, coming over. "Looking great. Very nice. Keep up the good work."

"Mrs Cooper?" says Amelia. "I've had an idea about the final song for the musical."

"Oh, yes?" Mrs Cooper is interested.

"Well, there's a song by Megan Flyer called 'Party Don't Stop' that I think would be perfect for a big finish. Also, Natalie Baker and I kind of half already have a dance for it. What do you think?"

"Sounds interesting. I'll probably need to hear the song first," replies Mrs Cooper.

"It's a *terrible* idea!" pipes up Harriet, unable to contain herself. "Mrs Cooper, the lyrics have nothing to do with our story. It's all about dancing around at a party in *America*. And this is a *British* production."

"*Hello?*" I say. "It's set in *Kansas*. In *America*. I'm very jealous of your intellect right now, Harriet."

"I've got it on my iPod if you want to listen?" Amelia says to Mrs Cooper.

"Well, yes, OK then." Mrs Cooper perches on the edge of the table and puts one of Amelia's earbuds in her ear.

She nods along to the music, and I have to stifle an urge to giggle. I don't really know why it's funny. I guess it's just that a middle-aged cardigan-wearing teacher like Mrs Cooper isn't exactly Megan Flyer's target market.

"Well, it's certainly a catchy tune," she says eventually and hands Amelia back the earbud. "What are the rest of the lyrics like? Is there any swearing in it?"

"No, there's no swearing," replies Amelia.

"There may be no swearing, but the lyrics are banal nonsense!" complains Harriet.

"I think they're relevant," argues Amelia politely. "It's the story of someone moving somewhere where they don't know anyone; they're scared, but then they go to a fun party and they relax and have fun, and suddenly they're not so scared any more."

"Well, that does *kind of* echo the theme of the *Wizard of Oz* a little bit," Mrs Cooper muses. "And you say this is a popular song? Do lots of the other pupils like it?"

"Yes," says Amelia.

"*No*," says Harriet. "Mrs Cooper, you can't allow this to happen. Our school will be a laughing stock.

It's a really terrible, vacuous pop song. It has nothing to do with the *Wizard of Oz* and no artistic merit whatsoever."

"What do you think, Jessica?" Mrs Cooper addresses me. "Is it popular with the other students?"

Hmmm. I appear to be the *adjudicator.* Well, *this* is an interesting turn up for the books. I mean, I don't massively care either way about the song. But I'd agree the finale should be "There's a Hole in My Bucket" if I thought it would annoy Harriet right now.

Ha! You're going *down*, Harriet.

"Oh yes. It's very popular," I reply. "*Everyone* our age likes it. Well, if they have any taste, of course. And I think it will be the *perfect* way to end the musical."

Amelia positively *beams* at me.

"Right! That's settled then," says Mrs Cooper. "I'll discuss it with the others, but I think this might be a great way to end the show. Well done, Amelia." And she's off again before Harriet can protest any further.

Chapter 10

Harriet sulks for the rest of the rehearsal and doesn't speak to either of us. (Which is an unexpected bonus. So really it's win/win.)

"Hey," says Amelia, once Harriet is gone. "Thanks *loads* for doing that. I didn't want to say that in front of *Her Majesty*."

"Ha, oh, you're welcome," I say.

"No, seriously, I really appreciate it," says Amelia earnestly. The most earnest I've ever seen her in fact. "And for the record, you are *not* stupid."

"Oh yeah, uh, I know," I say awkwardly.

I mean, I do know I'm not stupid. *Obviously*. But I am sometimes kind of lazy and easily distracted. Which sort of amounts to the same thing, grade wise.

But Auntie Joan says I have an *"inquisitive mind"* and that's a *"sign of intelligence"*. Plus, I still know the word *inalienable*. So I don't feel that bad about it.

"And I'm sorry I've called you stupid in the past," adds Amelia. Hang on. *Stop the press*. Amelia *never* apologises. (Unless Natalie makes her.) What's going on?

"Really?" I can't hide my surprise.

"I've been quite impressed by your professionalism, actually," Amelia continues in that blasé way she does. "I sort thought you were a dosser. You know, always joking, messing around. But you work *really hard* at Art. And you're actually *very competent*. I've, like, totally never seen you take work seriously before."

"Um … thanks?" I manage, confused.

"It's a shame Art isn't a *real* subject, in a way," adds Amelia, sounding sad for me. And there we go. I knew she'd have to undercut all this niceness somehow. "Otherwise you'd have quite a bright future ahead of you." OK, we can stop undercutting now, I think. *Enough.*

I don't exactly *love* Amelia. But I think I definitely hate Harriet more. Amelia and I kind of have an understanding: she only picks on me when she's really bored or in front of her "cool" friends. But since she and I have a very different idea of what constitutes "cool" it mainly doesn't really matter or bother me.

Anyway, it's nice to have a "win" against Harriet VanDerk. Especially after the bossiness, the paint fiasco and the calling me stupid.

Finally, I get to hang out with Natalie for a bit. I'm going to her house after rehearsal. Amelia tells Nat the good news about the end-of-musical song and dance on the bus.

"So, we should, like, totally practise," says Amelia, getting up for her stop.

"Yes, we should, but I'm very busy at the moment," says Nat. "It might be hard to fit in, but I'm sure we can."

"O-K," replies Amelia, looking slightly put out. We say our goodbyes.

"I thought you'd be more excited than

that," I say. "You love that song. You and Amelia spent *ages* making up that dance to go with it."

I remember, I was there when they made it up. I pressed "play" on the iPod dock.

It was a very important role.

"Oh, I *know*," enthuses Natalie. "I am really pleased."

"Now you actually get to perform it in front of people for real!" I say.

"Yes, I'm really glad. Did I not sound glad? I am. Truly. I think that just shows how tired I am, if I didn't sound that happy about it."

"Well, why are you so tired?" I ask.

"Oh Jess, I'm *exhausted*. This musical is really taking it out of me." She sighs dramatically. Oh great, *this* again.

"It's fun too, though, right?" I say. "I mean, you're still enjoying it and everything?"

"Oh God, yes!" exclaims Natalie. "It's some of the most fun I've ever had!" OK, now she's gushing.

"Charming!" I jokily fold my arms and pretend to be annoyed.

"Except for all the fun *we* have together," she adds grinning.

"I should think so, young lady." I fake-reprimand her. She affectionately shoves me on my arm, and then we get up for her stop.

Later, in Nat's bedroom, after a tasty dinner of her mum's delicious homemade chicken stew with French bread and butter, followed by trifle (I *know* – my family still have a long way to go) we lie on her bed, half doing our homework and half chatting.

Some of the chat is me saying things like, "What did you get for number six?" But Nat doesn't mind sharing answers, and sometimes I know the ones that she doesn't, so it *is* fair.

"Hey, Jess?" says Natalie suddenly.

"Yeah?"

"Do you think, um, do you think there might be any like, talent spotters in the audience?"

"Of our school musical?" I ask.

"Yeah."

"Um. Well, never say never," I reply, doubtfully. "But don't—"

"That would be *so cool*, wouldn't it?" she interrupts excitedly.

"Well, yeah, but—"

"Imagine if there were talent spotters from *Hollywood* in the audience!" Nat interrupts me again. "Wouldn't that be amazing?"

"It *definitely* would," I reply dryly. "Unbelievable, in fact."

Oh, dear. Poor Nat, she's starting to get totally carried away with this musical stuff. I mean, at least when I was planning world domination for our school comic, I was (a) half joking; and (b) prepared for it to take at least a few weeks.

Natalie is totally deluded if she thinks there are going to be Hollywood talent spotters in an audience made up chiefly of reluctant parents. I'm pretty sure no one's parents work for Hollywood at our school.

And just say there *was* someone in from Hollywood

who was a talent scout looking to be impressed –
they are obviously *far* more likely to be blown away
by the scenery and offer *me* a job in Hollywood. Ha
ha. I'm quids in.

Chapter 11

"Ready for this?" asks my dad, holding out the saucepan at dinner time on Sunday.

"*Si, si!*" replies Ryan, showcasing some Spanish he learned from a cartoon.

Taking my mum's guilt-speech to heart (the one where she pointed out quite accurately that she does the lion's share of things around here), my dad is trying to pull his weight a bit more.

 Unfortunately, the main meal in his repertoire is beans on toast. To get past how dull this would quickly become, my dad has cunningly added some Nando's Peri Peri hot sauce to the beans, and now he's

calling them "Mexican".

Ryan is buying it, and that's the main thing. "Tonight we're in Mexico," he tells Lady, who is lying loyally by his feet.

Bet my dad wishes he thought of this when we were deep in the economy drive. Just add spices to all our favourite cheap foods, and suddenly every night is international night.

My dad finishes dishing up and sits down. We all tuck in. It tastes a bit weird to be honest, but I suppose I like it.

"Thank you, I appreciate the *effort*," my mum tells him. Which I think, reading between the lines, means she doesn't *love* it.

"*Si, si*," says my dad happily. I think he must have learnt his Spanish from the same cartoon as Ryan. "*Andale, arriba*." (Now I'm sure of it.)

"Hello, family!" Tammy suddenly lets herself in through the back door, carrying her rucksack.

"Tammy, we're in the middle of dinner," says my mum, a bit put out.

"Smells weird, what is it?" asks Tammy.

"We're having Mexican beans on toast," explains

Ryan.

"A-ha," says Tammy. "Anyway, I've come to tell you—"

"Can this wait?" interrupts my mum. "We're having dinner. Come back in twenty minutes."

"I can't come back in twenty minutes," replies Tammy. "I'll be gone by then."

"Gone where?" I ask suspiciously.

"That's what I've to come to tell you. I've come to say goodbye."

"Where are you going?" asks my mum.

"I'm going…" Tammy pauses dramatically.

"Out with it!" My mum appears to be losing patience.

"Oh, sorry," replies Tammy sarcastically. "It's nothing. Just a little thing I call … *saving the planet*."

Tammy *always* tells us she's saving the planet. *Hey*, this might be a good opportunity to showcase my updating of the English language…

"Hey, Tammy, you sound like a *skipping iPod*!" I tell her. No one responds to me. It's like I haven't spoken.

"And how are you saving it *this* time?" Mum asks Tammy.

"The trees," replies Tammy cryptically.

"You tried to save some trees once before," says my mum. "Tied yourself to them, I believe. Made the paper if I recall."

"Oh, this is *nothing* like that," says Tammy dismissively. "This is *much* better organised. It's a proper sit-in. They've built tree houses and everything. There's a big team behind it, actually."

"Are you saving the forest from the bypass?" asks my dad, sounding awestruck.

"Yes, I am," says Tammy, proudly. "So I've just come to pick up a few things." She gestures to the rucksack. "Remember when I said about you guys providing a few snacks?"

She turns and starts taking our crisps from the cupboard and stuffing them into her rucksack.

"Hey, Tammy, watch it, those are *supermarket-brand* crisps!" I protest. Not your usual tat. "Why don't you just take the muesli bars from the back of the cupboard that no one ever eats?"

"Yeah, fine," says Tammy, though I'm not sure she's listening. I see her slip a couple of KitKats in there as well.

"That's enough now," says my mum.

"So this is goodbye for a while," says Tammy, zipping up her bag and slinging it over her shoulder. "I don't know how long I'll be gone, living under the stars. Maybe two nights, maybe two months. Just me, my friends and justice on our side."

"Amazing," mutters my dad, with a beatific smile.

"I think you're romanticising it a bit!" scoffs Mum.

"Am I? Or is it that next time you see me, I'll be a *hero*?" replies Tammy.

"I'm coming with you!" my dad blurts out, leaping to his feet.

"*What?*" laughs Mum.

"I'm going … under the stars … to save the birds. Trees!" garbles my dad excitedly.

"Very funny, Bert. Yeah, right, you're going to live up a tree." My mum chuckles. "Now sit down and finish your Mexican beans on toast."

"No! I'm doing it," says dad, frantically yet

apologetically. "I love you, kids. I love you, Janet. But this is something I must do." He pushes his chair back and takes a step towards Tammy.

"Um, Mum. Shouldn't you be stopping him?" I say quietly, starting to feel a little bit worried.

"Ha! *Stopping him*," scoffs Mum. "You go, Bert. Go on. You're welcome. You won't last the *night* in the great outdoors!"

Noooooo! My mum has just given my dad the classic sitcom vibe. CUT TO: Dad sitting in a tree a year later. No. This is not good.

"Oh, thank you!" says Dad earnestly. He bends and kisses Mum on the cheek. "You're a very understanding wife. I'll just grab a few things," he says to Tammy. "I probably need a coat. Hang on."

Tammy looks as shocked as me. I can see her working out how to play this. The thing is, her schtick is antagonism. And that kind of falls apart if anyone agrees with her. If my dad goes with her to save a forest, *she* is less special for doing it. He's totally stealing her thunder.

But she's going to have to pretend she's delighted. Even though she's about to be living together 24/7 with her (normally) straitlaced dad and her alternative hippy friends. Wait a minute – *there's* your sitcom!

"OK!" Dad comes back wearing his biggest coat and carrying a small overnight bag that I presume contains his toothbrush and stuff.

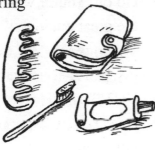

"Not saying I'm not delighted you've stepped up, Dad, but this is your last chance to change your mind," says Tammy warily.

"Yes, Bert, last chance!" chortles Mum. Why isn't Mum *stelping* ™ this?!

"I love you all," says Dad. "Take care of each other while I'm gone."

"*Whatever*. See you tomorrow!" Mum waves cheerily.

"Goodbye!" Dad calls over his shoulder from the back door as they leave.

"Enjoy weeing in a bucket!" Mum calls back.

"Mum! I can't believe you're letting him do this." The sound of the door slamming triggers the return of my power of speech. Ryan is still just staring at the space where his father used to be, his mouth open, a few Mexican beans dropping slowly off his fork.

"Oh, please." Mum waves a hand airily. "Have you *met* your father? He won't last the night. He'll be home tomorrow morning for his breakfast, you mark my words."

Chapter 12

CUT TO: I only have one parent at breakfast. Thank you *very much,* Mum, for being oblivious to how sitcoms work.

For a second I thought I heard my dad coming down the path, but it turned out to be the postman. (So I grabbed the post before Lady could.)

It wasn't a dream. My dad has gone to live up a tree. Who *does* that? What is *wrong* with him? I suppose he has been acting a *bit* funny lately. Almost as if he's having a mid-life crisis or something.

But come on. *Bert Morris* up a tree?

For one thing, he loves rules and laws and things like that. He thinks the world would fall apart if we only obeyed the rules we *liked.*

And he's all for *keeping up with the Joneses* (or in our case the VanDerks). You'd think the embarrassment about what the neighbours will say would deter him, even if nothing else would.

On the other hand, he really does care about birds, and wants to make a difference and save them. And I suppose he has been cooped up in an office for the last twenty years.

They say a change is as a good as a rest. And living up a tree is definitely quite a change from suburbia. Maybe it might even do him some good and make him happier.

I mean, he'll have to come home *eventually*, right? I'm not that worried, *really*. I'm ninety-five per cent sure Dad will come back soon. And I like those odds.

"You're not *serious*?" I'm trying to keep my voice down because there's a real danger I might shout at Joshua and Tanya otherwise. I think I've been pretty patient with them so far but this really takes the biscuit. And nobody likes a biscuit-taker. (Except maybe people with wheat allergies.)

They tell me at *break-time on Monday* that they can't make the Monday lunchtime comic meeting! That's just *rude* – lines to practise or no lines to practise.

"Can't be helped, Toons," says Tanya earnestly. I roll my eyes. I think it very much *can* be helped.

"Look, we're really sorry." Joshua *does* sound like he means it, to be fair. "This is the last time, I promise."

"You *keep* saying that," I reply.

"Don't be like that, Toons," says Tanya. "We're all friends here. We got to help each other out. This musical is the first time anyone's taken me seriously. I wanna do a good job and that."

I start to relent. Though, honestly, I thought *our comic* was the first time anyone took her seriously. She shouldn't just abandon it because a *better* serious thing has come along. Otherwise she's just a *user*. Exactly.

"Look." I address both of them. "You said you wanted to work on my Parents' Handbook idea *together* so I've waited to start that. It's wrong that you've stopped me working on it by myself if you haven't got time to do it. I could have been getting *loads* done. It could have been ready to go to print."

"I know," says Joshua guiltily.

"It's not fair. You wouldn't like this the other way round. Just because there's two of you doesn't mean it's OK."

"I know," says Joshua again. "It's just," he pauses, "if I can get this bit down, I can finally relax, and start enjoying the musical a bit more."

Well, obviously I don't want him to have a horrible time on the musical. Obviously.

"Yeah, Toons," agrees Tanya, sounding unusually humble for her.

"And I do still really want to work on the Parents' Handbook idea," says Joshua. "Please don't do it without me."

Ohhh. "Fine," I sigh wearily. "But this can't continue. If you leave me with just Lewis for input it's going to be a very Star Wars heavy issue." **SIGH**

Joshua allows himself a small chuckle. "I know. Honestly, this is the last time."

At lunchtime Amelia surprises me.

"Hey, um, Jessica? I was wondering if you wanted

116

to come round after school maybe tomorrow or Thursday and we could go through the dance, make sure we're happy with it? You know, before we have to teach it to other people."

"Oh, uh, really?" I say. (As I said, I was surprised. I've flagged that up already.)

"Yes, you know for the musical," she says. "So that it's *so good* that Harriet won't be able to find fault with it."

She's said the magic words. "Yes, definitely. I'd love to," I hear myself say. Anything to annoy Harriet.

I mean, actually I wouldn't *love* to. In fact, the idea of going round to Amelia's immaculate house without Natalie there to act as a sort of buffer kind of scares me a little. But it's for a good cause.

Joshua, Tanya, Natalie and some of the others are staying after school a tiny bit longer to rehearse on Monday night, but it's not an *official* rehearsal. Mrs

Cooper won't be there, so we're not doing any more artwork anyway.

Amelia is actually rehearsing her part as the good witch this time. So I'm getting the bus home on my own.

"Bye, guys, Nat!" I call out, waving to them on the stage. "Have fun!"

"What? Oh, right in the middle of something here, babes, I'll speak to you later!" calls out Nat, sort of dismissively.

"Yeah, that's what I'm saying!" I shout back. "I'm only saying goodbye and good luck!" I find it hard not to feel a tiny bit hurt and aggrieved by her response.

"You're interrupting us!" she calls back. "Laters!"

I can't be bothered to respond. *Well* fine, *Natalie*, I think sarcastically to myself as I get the bus home. *If that's how you want to be.*

Joshua calls me later on and suggests that we could have a comic meeting at the Slush Pile after school one day or if not, on Saturday. He seems genuinely sorry about missing stuff.

"So we'll confirm nearer the time, but probably Saturday," he says.

"Saturday," I agree.

"Yes. I mean, I will just double check with Tanya and stuff, but it should be fine. Basically if you don't hear from me, it's on. We're meeting on Saturday." He says this very firmly.

"Great," I reply.

Honestly, the amount of time Tanya, Joshua and me spend *scheduling* meetings, we could have easily *had* one by now. *Still*, I feel it would be mean to point this out when he seems to be really trying.

My dad has not returned home yet. But Mum is still being really blasé about it, so I'm ninety per cent sure he will be back soon.

Chapter 13

OK. At what point do I have to re-categorise Mum's attitude from "blasé" to "in denial"?

I don't think I'm catching the drama bug but it's Friday morning now. Dad has been away for *four* days.

Mum still just keeps saying it's "hilarious" but really, I think the joke is wearing kind of thin. Dad is pretty much calling her bluff now.

Then again, she has known him longer than I have, so maybe she is right? Either way I'm eighty-five per cent sure he probably *will* be home soon.

And I have a plan to help make that happen: basically, Ryan and I will go to see him at the weekend and tell him to come home. It's not much of a plan, I know.

And if that doesn't work, I'll call Auntie Joan and see what she thinks. (Obviously I can't call Tammy, seeing as she started all this.)

On Tuesday I told Nat I thought she'd been a bit dismissive of me the other day and she apologised. But then she almost immediately went back to acting kind of funny with me. Just being a bit rude and flippant. Like *she's* important and I'm ... well, *not*.

I'm still trying and (mainly) succeeding in being sympathetic to the pressure she feels under. And my jokes still seem to cheer her up. But I kind of thought she might calm down now she knows her lines better, but she hasn't. If anything, she's getting *worse*.

There is another after-school rehearsal on Friday that Amelia is not a part of. So this is the day I have agreed to go to her house to go over the dance.

Amelia and I swing by the hall to say goodbye to everyone. (Even if I *do* end up accused of *interrupting* – at least *I* am still *polite*.) "Break a leg!" I call out to Joshua and Tanya. "See you tomorrow!"

"What?" says Joshua, coming over.

"See you tomorrow," I repeat. "At the Slush Pile. For the comic meeting?"

"That isn't happening tomorrow," says Joshua.

"What's all this?" Tanya joins us. Amelia looks uncomfortable at Tanya's presence, but says nothing.

"Um. On Monday, when you rang me?" I prompt Joshua, but he looks nonplussed. "You said let's meet up on Saturday, at the slushie place?" I remind him.

"Oh, right. But, no, didn't we say we'd confirm it in the week?" he asks.

"Um, well…" I try to remember the conversation.

"No one confirmed it," says Joshua.

"Yeah," says Tanya.

"No, no. Wait, I remember now," I reply. "You said you wanted to double check it was good, but that it probably was, so if I didn't hear back from you, assume it was on." That is nearly *word for word* what he said. He is *not* getting out of this.

"Well, look, I'm really sorry but it sort of slipped my mind," says Joshua.

"You have *got* to be kidding me!" I snap. "Come *on*, Joshua."

"He never confirmed it, Toons," says Tanya defensively.

"Yeah, but he never *unconfirmed* it, either," I say. "That's his *own* rule. We had it in the diary, and if you couldn't do it, you should have said. Please don't tell me you guys are cancelling *another* meeting. You *promised*."

"We're not cancelling," says Joshua.

"So you'll be there?" I say.

"No. We can't," says Joshua. "But we're not cancelling. There's been a mix-up."

"Honest mistake, Toons," adds Tanya.

"Oh my *God*," I blurt out. "Technicalities aside, why aren't you coming to this meeting?"

"We've told you," says Joshua.

"You guys are *unbelievable*!" I retort. Then, "Come on, Amelia." We start turning to go, and I add, "Enjoy your *precious* acting, since apparently it's the only thing that *matters*!"

"Hey, hey!" Natalie is suddenly calling after us, so

we sort of have to stop after a few paces of our *storm out*. "Where are you two going?"

"We're going to my house to go through the dance," says Amelia.

"Oh." Natalie appears to take this in for a second. "Why didn't you ask *me*?" She sounds a tiny bit shocked.

"I *did*," says Amelia crossly. "I've been asking you *all week*. You keep saying you're too busy."

"That's not the point." Nat falters a little.

"Isn't it?" I ask, my patience short now. "Aren't you rehearsing right now anyway? You couldn't have come."

"You should still have – I mean, if I'd known you were actually doing it anyway, I could have tried to come," says Nat.

"Well, would you like to come over after you've finished rehearsing?" asks Amelia patiently.

"Oh, yeah, you'd *like* that, wouldn't you?" says Nat, perplexingly.

"Yes, we would," I reply factually. In all the annoyance, I'd forgotten how intimidated I am at the prospect of going to Amelia's house by myself.

"Well, I just think it's really mean that you two are

trying to exclude me," says Natalic.

Well, doesn't *that* just take *all of the biscuits ever in the whole world*? I'm starting to see red. That could *not* be more *rich* coming from Natalie! I mean *PLEASE* – does she *really* want to start a dialogue with me about what it feels like to be *excluded*? After everything she and Amelia did before?

"Especially," Natalie adds, "when I'm under all this pressure."

That *does* it. "No one is excluding you!" I snap. "I'm kind of like the expert on how that feels, remember, and I can assure you, we're not forming a *secret gang* or anything, so you really don't need to worry."

"Why are you bringing up *ancient history*?" cries Nat.

I sort of already want to say I'm sorry and I didn't mean it, but what comes out is: "Just trying to say it's not all about *you*, Nat."

"Oh!" Then Natalie seems to have a revelation. "I *knew* it, you're both jealous I got the lead part and you're punishing me. You're trying to make me jealous, aren't you?"

"OK we're, like, totally not doing that," says Amelia.

"I didn't even audition," I say.

Nat is looking at us and shaking her head, as if she can't quite believe what is happening to her.

"Guys, this is really silly," says Amelia, the voice of reason (for a change). "You two are totally best friends. I think tensions are running high because of the musical and everything. And I think you should both shake hands and agree to be friends, and everything will seem better in the morning."

Stunned, Nat and I grudgingly shake hands. Amelia and I leave. Time was that Amelia was *trying* to split Nat and me up, and she would have revelled in that argument, picking and stirring at it and making it worse.

But now she has saved us from saying even more horrible things to each other. Have I *misjudged* Amelia all this time?

Going to Amelia's house turns out to be more fun than I thought it would be.

"Come on, Jessica. You have to learn it, too." Amelia is trying to drag me away from my old role of pressing "play" on the iPod dock.

"I'm really not one of life's dancers," I explain.

I've been to Amelia's house quite a few times with Nat. Even with her calming presence, I'm normally terrified I'll spill Ribena or something on to one of the thick cream rugs.

But this time, weirdly, I feel slightly more relaxed. Maybe it's because I'm so cross with Joshua, Tanya and Natalie that I don't have room in my head to worry about the cream rugs.

Amelia has practised the dance on her own and is satisfied she knows it like the back of her hand. But I still don't see why that means I have to have a go.

"Look," she says seriously. "What if I'm sick one day? If we can both do it, Harriet will have less chance of stopping us." And I can't really argue with that.

As I stand up, waiting for the music, I feel really self-conscious, and like an idiot. But as I have to concentrate to remember the moves, I forget to feel embarrassed and throw myself into it. It starts to be … fun.

Amelia steps in to correct a couple of the things I am doing wrong, like I'm not lifting my arms high enough at one point. But eventually she says I am definitely good enough to teach other people. Ha! Who would have thought *that* could happen?

"The bits where you forget to be self-conscious are really good," Amelia tells me at the end. "You just have to believe in yourself more."

Whoa. Whoa. Whoa. Just a minute here. *Amelia* has just told *me* to *believe* in myself! What is going on?!

When I get home there is still no sign of Dad. But I'm not worried. I'm still eighty per cent sure he will be back soon.

Mum seems to be finding it less funny now, which is sort of a relief but also a bit weird.

Never mind. Ryan and I will bring him home tomorrow. I'm seventy-five per cent sure of that.

Chapter 14

"Hurry up, Ryan!" I call upstairs to my little brother on Saturday morning. Without even having to see him, I add, "No bat, no Winnie the Pooh, and no space helmet on you *or* the dog."

"But she *likes* it!" Ryan protests from the landing. Weirdly, Lady *does* seem to sort of like her makeshift, cardboard-box space helmet. Or at least she doesn't *mind* it. But that's neither here nor there. I'm not taking them out looking like that.

"Any messages for Dad?" I ask my mum before

we leave. "Do you want to come actually?" I bet my mum could *shout* him down out of that tree.

"Tell him…" Mum thinks, "tell him I'm impressed with his staying power, but he's made his point. It's getting a bit silly now. But if he *wants* to be silly and stay up there, that's fine."

Well, I think. I'll tell him *some* of that. I might have to re-write it a bit, so it sounds like a *direct instruction*. I don't want to berate my mum for her tragic lack of sitcom knowledge but I'm pretty sure that if she watched a bit more TV this would never have happened.

When we get to Deanbury Forest, Ryan, Lady and I make our way through the tents and protesters towards the trees. It's all starting to feel a bit more real.

We pass some diggers and see where construction has started and then stopped. There's a big, ugly, brown gash in the otherwise beautiful scenery.

What my dad is doing is actually a proper … *thing*, rather than an abstract ideal.

Near the horrible gash of uplifted earth are some men in work clothes, just standing around. I guess it's just another day where they can't really do anything. Some policemen stand near them, not doing anything either. Ryan and I veer away from them.

There are quite a few rudimentary tree houses in the branches. It takes us a while to find Dad. But a couple of protesters point us in the direction of "Bert Morris's tree" and so finally we do.

"Dad! Daaaaaad! Are you up there? It's Ryan and Jessica!" I shout. Lady barks for good measure.

"Kids? *Ryan! Jessica!*" My dad's excited voice shouts back. We look up at the tree and see a familiar but now stubble-covered face peer over the edge of the tree house.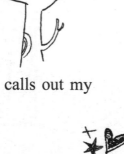

"Hi!" I call out, waving.

"Daddy! You're growing a beard!" exclaims Ryan.

"Yes, I can't really shave up here," calls out my

dad, rubbing his face with his hand.

"Do you think you'll be down soon?" I ask him.

"I'm sorry, I can't come down yet," says Dad.

"Not even to chat?" I ask. "We have to keep shouting up at you?"

"Afraid so!" he replies.

"What if we say please with a capital P?" asks Ryan.

"Sorry! What I'm doing is very important!" replies my dad.

"What *are* you doing?" asks Ryan.

"Your dad is being a hero!" comes another voice, and another beardy face appears in the tree.

"Like Batman and Spiderman?" asks Ryan.

"Uh … yes!" answers the new voice. "Your dad is saving this forest like a superhero in a comic!

Except, he doesn't have superpowers, so it's going to take him a bit longer than it would Batman."

"That figures!" I call out sarcastically. "How *much* longer?"

"Are you Jessica?" calls out new beardy face. "I'm Jay Bowman! Your dad's told me all about you kids. Did you come up with the nickname *Environator*? We've all been chuckling about that." Have they indeed? *Charming.* Doesn't he know there is meant to be no judgment in blue sky?

"Excuse me!" pipes up Ryan, evidently feeling left out. "I'm called Ryan. And Batman doesn't have any superpowers anyway."

"Hello, Ryan!" Jay chuckles. "Quite right. But he has loads of gadgets. We don't have any of those."

"And you don't even have a cape!" Ryan responds, making Jay and my dad laugh.

"Yeah, they've really dropped the ball on this superhero business," I comment, although I am starting to feel secretly impressed that my dad is part of this huge thing, trying to make a difference.

"Can we come up?" asks Ryan.

"That's probably not a good idea," shouts Dad. "It's a bit grim up here, to be honest. I don't think you'd like it."

"Daddy, how do you go to the toilet up there?" asks Ryan.

"You don't want to know!" answers Dad.

I think that Ryan probably really does, but fortunately he changes tack. "How do you get food up there?" he asks.

"Oh, people bring us things to eat."

"How do you have a bath?"

"Well, there's no bath as such, we—"

"And how do you brush your teeth?" Ryan interrupts.

"Stop asking Dad so many questions!" I snap at him. "You're not even listening to the answers."

"Daddy, *are* you brushing your teeth?" Ryan demands obstinately.

"Kind of!" comes the reply. "Sometimes we get brought a bucket of water, and we can have a bit of a wash and brush our teeth then."

"That sounds gross," proclaims Ryan.

"It's really not so bad, when you get used to it,"

says dad brightly. "And the best times are at night. You can see all the stars so clearly, and we all sing songs."

My dad sounds genuinely happy up there, like some kind of giant boy scout, really enjoying his camping trip. He's remarkably adaptable for a fusty middle manager who likes his car clean and his lawn neat. (Not that they ever really are.)

"Can you sing me one of the songs?" asks Ryan.

"Actually I'm not sure that I can, Ryan, some of the words are a bit rude," replies dad.

So now he's singing sweary *anarchist* songs, is he? Why did he ever bother living in a house at all? He's clearly a *wild* giant boy scout. Is that even a thing? I'm not sure.

"I've missed you both a lot," says Dad, more sadly.

"We've missed you!" I reply.

"And Lady has," adds Ryan. "And Mum! She's sent you a message!"

"Oh yes?" calls out Dad.

This is it. This is my moment to convince him to come home. What was I going to say again? Mum is angry … and… But as I look up into my dad's face, I realise I can't really lie to him.

And I don't want to *force* him to give up doing something he believes in. (Even though *he* has been perfectly happy to force *me* to eat mushy peas in the past.) I guess I'm the bigger person. I am *Robert Wadlow*.

"She said she was impressed with your staying power!" I shout up at him. Dad beams. "She also also thinks you're being silly, but that if you *want* to be silly then stay up there." Dad laughs, but looks ever so slightly choked up.

"I do want to be silly," he replies, more quietly.

"I wish you could come home," I say.

"I know. Me, too. But I'm doing this for you! You and your children, and your children's children. And the birds. And the birds' children, and—"

"OK, we get it!" I interrupt.

"Daddy, we're running a bit low on KitKats!" says Ryan then.

"Well, there isn't much I can do about that from up here, Ryan!" replies Dad.

"*Daddy, please!*" whines Ryan. "You're supposed to!"

"Do not *whine*, Ryan!" instructs Dad crossly. "I may be living up a tree, but I am still your father and you have to do what I say!"

I decide we'd better take this as our cue to leave. Ryan is quick to forgive, though, and natters about how Dad is a hero all the way home.

"And Daddy will be thinking of us lots, and missing us, but it's for the greater good, so that we have a nicer future, and so will all the other children too. Our dad is saving everyone, not just us, Jess. Aren't we lucky?"

He rambles on, jumping over rocks and sticks, with Lady bounding along next to him.

"Yes, we're very lucky," I reply dutifully.

But then I start to wonder if, actually, maybe we *are*? I mean, my dad is at least displaying a *can-do* attitude. Maybe he is a really good role model? He's following his dreams, after all.

And, actually, so are Natalie, Joshua and Tanya. It's just that their dreams are stopping them from hanging out with *me*.

Well, maybe I should start following *my* dreams, too? But *how*? Everyone's gone off after theirs and left me behind, dreamless.

As I lie in bed later that night, I feel a bit like the world has turned upside down. Look what's been happening:

1. My strait-laced, law-abiding dad is living up a tree.

2. My normally grounded and level-headed best friend has become a diva.

3. I've actually had *fun* dancing to a pop song.

4. Amelia, my own private bully and *Fremenis*™ has earnestly told me to believe in myself.

The world has clearly gone mad. It's *not* me, it's *them*. But I still feel a bit sad and bewildered before I drift off to sleep.

⟹

In the morning I don't feel sad and bewildered any more. I feel energised and righteous. I love how sleep can do that sometimes.

Who cares what Natalie, Tanya and Joshua are up to? I don't need them. I don't need anyone. I'm not waiting any more for everyone to spare me some of their *precious* time. I'll do what I always do: draw something. That's what I'm good at.

And I know what my dream is. Right now it's to write funny stuff for my Parents' Handbook idea. So that's what I'm going to do. *Ha*.

After breakfast, I sit at my desk and start jotting down ideas of what could be funny advice for parents. It's *fun*.

Things like:

1. Never say no to your child in front of their friends. Same goes for asking them if they need a wee.

2. A 15 certificate is just a guideline.

3. If you are bad at cooking and insist on serving your kids soggy fish fingers, at least be prepared to provide a financial incentive and remunerate them accordingly.

4. Toys R Us is for life, not just for Christmas. Take regular trips there.

5. Harry Potter World is *not* "too expensive for what it is". Same goes for Chesington World of Adventures and Alton Towers.

6. What's more important, that carpet or your child's self-esteem? Exactly, thought so. No shouting about accidents.

7. No shouting in general.

8. Always ask your children if they *want* to go to relatives' boring weddings. If they say no, respect their wishes. Don't force the issue. And certainly don't make them wear horrible dresses or bow ties.

9. Always buy your children sweets.   I t makes them happy. And if they're happy, *you're* happy.

Suddenly I hear a smashing noise coming from the living room. Ryan and I rush downstairs just in time to see Lady bolting from the scene of the crime.

My mum enters from the kitchen, carrying a tea towel. "What the – ?" She stops as she sees a broken vase lying smashed on the floor. "Did that blimmin' dog do that?"

"No!" Ryan shouts instantly. "It was me, Mummy. I was running in the house again when I shouldn't have been."

Ryan, you hero, I think silently. I want to argue and say I did it, but then my mum will know we're lying.

"Oh Ryan, *why*?" My mum suddenly looks very

tired.

"I wasn't thinking," says my selfless little brother.

"I'm really upset with you, Ryan. I don't need this today." She looks genuinely sad having to rebuke him, though. But I guess rules is rules.

"I'm really sorry, Mummy," says Ryan. "You can take it out of my pocket money." Even though we don't exactly spend in the fast lane, I'm pretty sure the vase cost more than his moneybox holds.

"Well, I think you'd better go to your room," says my mum. That's not *too* bad a punishment. That's where Ryan was just playing anyway.

I help my mum clear up the broken vase, chatting incessantly about how Ryan didn't mean to do it and how it could have happened to anyone.

Back at my desk, I add to my Parents' Handbook advice:

10. Vases, like promises, are made to be broken.

I consider adding something about how under no circumstances should you have a mid-life crisis and go and live up a tree, but I'm worried it might be too specific to me and therefore niche.

I go through my list, to see if I can phrase it any differently and make it even funnier. Then I start illustrating it with cartoons.

I lose track of time until I hear Ryan calling, "Can I come out now?"

Mum says no, so I go and get him a KitKat.

"Here you go, Ryan," I say. "It was really brave of you to take the blame for Lady."

"Yes," says Ryan proudly, happily taking the KitKat.

"I'll take the next one so it's fair," I tell him.

"OK," says Ryan with his mouth full. "And then I'll bring you a KitKat."

"Deal," I reply. And we shake on it.

Chapter 15

By the time it's school on Monday, I'm feeling a lot more Zen about everything. I'm really pleased with my Parents' Handbook ideas, Mum and Ryan are friends again and everything feels more peaceful.

I've got the whole acting thing in perspective, and I'm looking forward to showing Joshua and Tanya my new work. I'm sure they'll like it and it will spur us all on to work harder at the comic again.

Natalie is a bit frosty with me at first but by the end of the day she seems to be more or less normal again.

Before the after-school rehearsal starts (and I get *too* sidetracked by painting and designing) I go over to Tanya and Joshua to show them my ideas.

"Hey, how are my favourite thespians?" I say.

"What did you call me?" asks Tanya, looking a bit lairy.

"Relax, it means actor," says Joshua.

"Actually, it means *tragic actor*," I correct. (There has to be some upside to hanging out with Harriet VanDerk.) "And you guys are pretty tragic," I joke.

"Oi," says Tanya, but she grins. Tanya doesn't mind being insulted if she thinks it's funny.

"The *Wizard of Oz* is hardly a tragedy," says Joshua.

"Not *usually*," I agree.

He chuckles. "So I take it this *hilarious* banter means you've forgiven us for not coming to comic meetings?"

"Yeah," I say. "Sorry if I overreacted. I just think it was all getting a bit silly. So I hope you don't mind, but I've taken matters into my own hands."

"Meaning?" Joshua raises an eyebrow. I don't know why he still thinks he's so cool. Especially when he's wearing a scarecrow hat.

"I've basically made the Parents' Handbook without you." I hold out my work just as Natalie comes over.

"Hey, that's good that is, Toons," says Tanya, leafing through it.

"Uh, what are you doing?" asks Nat, a bit aggressively.

"Um." I falter, taken aback. "Showing Joshua and Tanya some comic stuff."

"Well, you're stopping them rehearsing," she replies tersely.

"Nat, is this about the other day?" I ask.

"I don't know what you're talking about," she says airily. "But as you and Amelia pointed out, everyone's *very busy*, so it seems a bit rich to take up crucial rehearsal time for something else."

"*Seriously*, you're—" I try and interject.

"No, no, that's the rules, isn't it?" trills Nat. "I had to rehearse, so off you went with Amelia – well, now *they* have to rehearse, so you'd better skedaddle."

"Nat—"

"See how *you* like it!" she snaps. Then she just stands there with her arms folded. At least she seems to have finished talking.

"You're being totally unreasonable," I tell her, surprisingly calmly. The thing is, I *know* she is. I *know* this isn't me this time.

Joshua and Tanya look a tiny bit awkward. "Well, actually, we probably should get on, Jess," says Joshua gently.

"Yeah, *me too*," I say crossly. "I've got loads of set design to do. I was going to take up literally two seconds of your precious *actor time*."

"Oh well, guess we better stick to the schedule," says Nat. "Or maybe you can go off with Amelia or something?"

That's *it*. I cannot believe the audacity of the girl. I just turn and walk away from them without saying anything. I feel hot and embarrassed and angry. And I'm pretty sure that none of it is *my fault*. I'm really sick of this stupid musical now.

The rest of the rehearsal is *awful*. And only partly because Harriet VanDerk has started an official

146

protest against the Megan Flyer song and dance routine.

It's become a point of principle. The battle lines are drawn. Harriet on one side, Amelia and me, and, well, *wider society*, on the other.

"Hello, Megan." Harriet comes up to Megan, Fatimah and me, as we're making the flowers for Munchkinland.

"I'll get you! And your little dog, too!" shouts Tanya from the stage. (I can't believe I used to enjoy that line. I've heard it *waaay* too many times now.)

"Er, hi," replies Megan.

"Would you like to sign my petition?" asks Harriet.

"What's it for?" asks Megan.

"Ooh, are you trying to save the dolphins?" says Fatimah, somewhat optimistically, I think.

"It's to change 'Party Don't Stop' being the finale for the musical," says Harriet.

You can tell it irks her to have to say the song title out loud – the incorrect grammar is really painful for her. She's itching to put a comma after "party" – so it'd be an instruction: "Party, don't stop" rather than an observation about how long the party is going on for.

"Yeah!" says Megan excitedly, and starts singing.

"Love that song!" exclaims Fatimah. They both dance around for a bit.

"What were you saying?" asks Megan.

"Never mind." Harriet sighs and skulks off.

"No!" cries Nat from the stage. "We're not going anywhere until you help us!"

Typical *Natalie, trying to get her own way by arguing with the Wizard of Oz*, I think to myself dryly. *Huh, no wonder she's so good, she doesn't even have to* act. BOOM. (Just mentally high-fiving myself for that one.)

Chapter 16

I'm still seething when I get home, only to find that things are starting to crumble a tiny bit there too. My mum has been through several phases over the whole My-Husband-Lives-In-a-Tree situation: (1) laughter/denial; (2) Blitz spirit; and (3) martyrdom.

This last one is the current phase.

Ryan and I have been secretly keeping everything super tidy. Like moving breakables, shoes and piles of post out of the way so that Lady can't chew them. But then my mum had a panicky five minutes where she couldn't find the post.

"Ryan, *what* are you doing?" demands my mum suddenly.

I turn around from pushing the glasses further

back in the cupboard, and see that Ryan has just accidentally set the kitchen table for four instead of three.

"Oh, yeah," says Ryan, realising his mistake.

"You're not thinking!" she scolds.

"Hey, calm down, Mum, it was just an accident," I say. "Would you like a cup of tea?"

She sighs. "Yes, please, Jessica," she replies. "Sorry, Ryan poppet."

Ryan clears away the extra cutlery, I make the tea and my mum serves us up the tuna pasta bake. We sit down to eat.

"Thanks for the tea, love," says my mum, taking a sip.

"You're welcome." I relax and Ryan and I start eating.

"Eurrgh, what *is* this?" Mum suddenly gasps, nearly spitting tea out everywhere.

"It's a cup of tea, obviously," I reply.

"Jess, you have to do more than just *show* the tea bag the water, you know!"

"Sorry," I say.

"It's OK." She sighs again. "Your dad made a

cracking cup of tea."

"*Makes*, Mum," I correct. "He's coming back soon. I'm seventy per cent sure of that."

"Well, I hope he makes it quick," says my mum. "I'm all for him expressing himself and getting whatever this is out of his system, but he's using up all his holiday, you know."

"Well, at least it's for a good cause," I reply.

"But I wanted us to all go to Blackpool." My mum looks a bit forlorn. She loves Blackpool.

It's a shame the cup of tea I made didn't cheer her up. One of the downsides to my dad being away is definitely that there's no one here to make the all-calming tea.

Suddenly the back door opens and Tammy blunders in.

"Tammy!" exclaims Mum, surprised.

"Aren't you meant to be up a tree?" I ask.

"Where's Daddy?" demands Ryan.

"Oh yeah, he's still up there. He won't come down," she replies breezily.

"Um … how come *you've* come down?" I ask.

"Oh," says Tammy airily. "Well, I was needed on the ground, you know. Running errands, relaying messages. I'm *too useful* to be stuck up a tree, you know?"

Ha! Yeah, right! I think. Mum isn't buying it, either. She raises an eyebrow and looks like she's trying not to smirk.

"Are you sure it wasn't just that being up a tree with no toilet and lots of singing is a complete *nightmare*?" I tease.

"I can't believe you would say that to me!" Tammy is affronted.

"Would you like some dinner?" asks Mum.

"Oh, yes please," replies Tammy meekly and immediately slumps on to a chair. It seems Ryan *should* have laid the table for four after all. Maybe *he's* the psychic.

"I'm afraid this has tuna in it," says Mum. "You're still veggie, I assume?"

"Yes," says Tammy miserably.

"I could make you some toast?" offers Mum. "Or—"

"Oh, don't go to any trouble, Mum, I'll just eat

round it," cuts in Tammy.
And with that she moves a
tiny sliver of tuna fish to the side of the plate and
starts ravenously tucking in.

⇨

Eurrgh. School. Tuesday. Whose idea was Tuesday?
I am not impressed, whoever it was.

Natalie is now ignoring me! This is so ridiculous.
I can't believe how much she has blown everything
out of all proportion.

I eat lunch with Cherry and Shantair,
my chess-club friends. Shantair is the
cowardly lion and yet you don't hear *her*
going on about the musical non-stop. Well, she's
mentioned it a couple of times, but nothing as often
as Natalie.

The whole day is a massive drag that seems to take
for ever. Finally it's the rehearsal, and even that isn't
much fun because out of the corner of my eye I can
see Natalie dancing down the yellow brick road in
the background. Or singing and shouting
with the rest of the cast. And it keeps
reminding me that we're not speaking
and then I feel weird.

"Those flowers are looking wicked, Jess," enthuses Emily, as we continue to work on the flowers for Munchkinland.

"Cheers," I reply, trying to sound more ebullient than I feel.

"Emily," says Harriet formally, approaching us.

"Can I help you?" asks Emily.

"Yes. Would you like to sign my petition?" Harriet replies.

I'm really impressed with myself. I manage not to roll my eyes, or to punch Harriet in the face.

"That depends," says Emily suspiciously. "What's it for?"

"It's about the Megan Flyer song at the end of the musical," explains Harriet.

"Oh, *yeah*! 'Party Don't Stop'!" sings Emily, dancing a bit. "I didn't know you liked Megan Flyer, Harriet! Good on you!" Emily carries on dancing and sort of nudges Harriet, as if Harriet might want to join in. I can't help laughing.

"No, it's – *never mind*!" Harriet snaps and leaves in a huff.

"What happened?" asks Emily, genuinely surprised

by Harriet's reaction. She looks confused as I carry on laughing.

"I don't know," I reply. "But you've really cheered me up, Emily."

"Ha!" Emily looks pleased, and goes back to dancing. "Party don't stop!" I guess she thinks it's the song that's cheered me up. Oh, how wrong she is!

At least the day is nearly over. And on the plus side I *am* really pleased with how the flowers are looking.

Hmmm. You know it's probably not been a great day at school when that's the most positive thing you can say about it.

Chapter 17

At least my mum has some good news for us that evening. "Auntie Joan might be coming to visit us soon," she announces.

"Hurray!" says Ryan. **HURRAY !**

"Brilliant!" I agree. "Is she in town again with the orchestra?"

"No, she, uh, has some holiday to use up, and fancied coming to visit us for a bit."

"That's awesome!" I say. Now I don't have to ring her and tell her all the crazy stuff that's been going on. "It's nice she wants to spend her holiday with us," I add.

"Yes," agrees Mum. "Well, to be honest, when I told her about what your dad's been up to, she burst

out laughing and said she wanted to see for herself."
She pauses. "But I think she *mainly* wants to spend
her holiday with us," she adds quickly.

Hmmm.

"We got the official green light for the Megan Flyer
dance!" Amelia gushes to me as Harriet and I are
painting the grey bricks of the wicked witch's castle
(which *I* designed – thank you, thank you very much).

"That's great!" I say. "High five!"

Amelia and I high five (even though Amelia *never*
high fives because she thinks she's above it but *I* think
it's more she just never realised how fun it could be).

"I can't believe I just high-fived you," Amelia
giggles.

"Nor can I," says Harriet disdainfully.

"It's a shame no one signed your petition, Harriet,"
simpers Amelia.

Harriet's bid to stop a "vacuous" pop song from
"ruining" the musical has officially failed. Literally
no one signed it except her parents.

Harriet has chosen to put this down to "young
people not being interested in politics". But I think
it was probably Harriet's unpopularity coupled with

the killjoy nature of the petition.

Harriet is clearly annoyed but trying to remain superior. "Well, there's no accounting for taste," she replies loftily.

"Yeah, *yours*," scoffs Amelia. "And your parents'. Did you know your mum rang my mum to try to get me to drop it? *Unbelievable.* Your mum sounded like a right piece of work, too."

"Hey," I say suddenly.

"What?" asks Amelia.

"I, um, I just think it's important that no one is judged for what their *parents* do," I say. "You know, that's not fair."

"Her mum *rang* my mum about a pop song," says Amelia. "That's crazy."

"Yeah but that's not Harriet's fault." (I can't quite believe I'm saying this.)

"Unless she told her to," points out Amelia, "to get her own way."

"OK," I reply. "But let's just say parents are off limits. You know? Let's agree to be nice about Harriet's crazy parents, and then if any of our parents do something crazy ... like ... say, for example ... oh, I don't know ... go and live up a tree for a bit—"

"That's pretty crazy," interrupts Amelia.

"Exactly," I say, faltering slightly. "Then no one's allowed to comment on it."

"Um … OK," says Amelia.

"Harriet?" I query. But Harriet says nothing.

"Harriet?" says Amelia, more sternly. "Why aren't you agreeing to this? It's for your own protection."

"Agree in front of witnesses," I add.

"Fine," sighs Harriet. *Phew!*

"A verbal contract is binding in a court of law," I remind them, for good measure.

We get through the rest of the rehearsal fairly uneventfully. I think the wind has been taken out of Amelia's sails a little bit because she wanted to gloat about the song a bit more, and mock the overbearing VanDerk seniors, but I've kind of blocked her bullying.

But I think that's a good thing. Amelia's desire to make nasty comments about people is still the thing I like least about her. And when she can't do it any more, she puts her energy into other stuff and becomes way nicer.

As we start packing up our stuff at the end of

the session, Amelia comes over to me. "Would you like to come rollerskating with me on Saturday?" she asks.

"Um, really?" I say. Is this a *trick*? She used to trick me like this all the time. And rehearsing the song is one thing. But this sounds like a purely *social* event.

"Really." Amelia nods.

"What about Nat?" I ask. "Is she coming?" Maybe it's some plot to get us back together. Which would actually be sort of nice.

"No. I asked her, but she says she's too busy with the musical," says Amelia. "Actually, she's being a bit off with me at the moment."

"Me, too," I say. It's probably quite obvious given that we've barely spoken all week. I cough nervously. "I don't know if I can come," I reply. "I'll have to check."

Amelia raises an eyebrow. "I'm not tricking you, Jessica, if that's what you think."

"I haven't said that," I reply. Have *thought* it quite hard, though. But it's still not the same.

"Jessica, I am genuinely sorry I used to … bully you," says Amelia, obviously not wanting to use that word but not able to find a nicer replacement. "It's probably obvious, but I was jealous of you and Natalie when I was new at this school. Natalie was my only friend at first, and I thought the best way of keeping her would be to … get rid of you a bit."

Oh my God – she's admitted it!

"Riiight," I say, as nonchalantly as I can.

"Look, I'm not going to say I didn't know what I was doing, because I did. I did know I was bullying you. But I feel really embarrassed about it now. And I'm sorry."

This is amazing!

"I can't believe you've admitted it," I say.

"I know," she replies, smiling wryly. "I'm very brave."

I can't help but laugh. "You know, you should totally use your powers for good instead of evil," I say.

"Well, I *might* do that," replies Amelia. "One day."

I chuckle.

"I thought we were actually getting on," says Amelia.

"We are," I agree.

"Look. None of my regular friends are free much at the moment," admits Amelia. "And I get the feeling yours aren't, either."

Well, she has sort of got me there. And she did tell me to *believe in myself* the other day.

"OK," I say. "I would love to come rollerskating on Saturday."

"Are you *sure*?" queries Amelia, possibly aware she may have just talked me into it against my will.

"Of course I'm sure," I reply. "Don't be D.A.F.T."

"I'm going to let that one go," says Amelia.

"Probably wise," I reply.

And so ends one of the weirdest conversations I've ever had.

I wonder briefly if Nat will be annoyed with me when she hears about this. I mean, I'm literally doing exactly what she accused me of. But then she *has* been invited, too. Not that that has ever stopped her complaining.

And anyway, she keeps stopping Joshua and

Tanya from doing stuff with me. You know what? Maybe *I'm* annoyed with *her*. So maybe I don't need to *care* about what she thinks. Maybe that will serve her right.

Chapter 18

"Coooeee! Anybody home?"

"Auntie Joan!" squeals Ryan, taking a run at her legs as she drops her bags in our hallway on Saturday morning.

"How long are you staying, Joan, a month?" asks my mum, staring at all the luggage.

"Hey, there!" Joan hugs each of us in turn. "Hello, Lady, hello, gorgeous." She strokes our excited dog, whose wagging tail makes our hallway feel even more cramped. "Now, how about a nice cup of tea? Who's hungry?"

"I haven't got much in, I'm afraid," says my mum.

"You look exhausted," Joan replies.

"Well, I still need to go shopping," says my mum.

"No, no, no," says Joan firmly. "The fantastic Auntie Joan is here now. Why don't you have a nice relaxing bath and I can take the kids to the supermarket? They can tell me what we need to buy, can't you, kids?"

Ryan and I nod vigorously. This is basically *Dream Scenario One* for us.

"That would be amazing, actually," says my mum. "I haven't had a break from them for goodness knows how long, if you don't count work."

(Charming! Who would need a break from *us*? We're angels!) "Let me get my wallet."

"No, no," says Joan. "I'll get the shopping. My treat. What are sisters for?" (*Hmmm*. Tammy owes me and Ryan some quality snacks if *that's* what sisters are for.)

"Thanks, Joan," says Mum.

"Come on, kids," says our aunt, opening the front door. "Now, is Bert really up a tree?"

"Yes, but *shhhh*!" replies Mum. "We don't need

the neighbours to hear."

"Oh heavens, no," says Joan sarcastically. "It's the most impressive thing he's ever done!" she shouts into the front garden, teasing my mum. "I didn't know he had it in him."

"Just go!" Mum pushes us out and closes the front door firmly behind us.

➡

"So let me get this straight," says Joan, as we pull into the supermarket car park. "Your parents explicitly told you not to come home *without* loads of pizza and ice-cream?"

Ryan and I giggle. "It's their main rule of parenting," I joke. "They're really strict about it, Auntie Joan. We don't want to disobey them."

Joan chuckles and turns off the engine. "OK, kids. I'm happy to buy you all the junk food you want. We'll get some fruit and veg as well to keep your mum happy, but I think it's time we all enjoyed life a bit, don't you?"

All I can say is: *best shopping trip EVER*. Ryan and I fling Pop Tarts, doughnuts, samosas, fizzy drinks, sausages, cupcakes, sweets, pizzas, ice-cream, KitKats and even *Walkers* crisps into the

trolley. It's basically like Christmas, but in May, and we get to choose the menu. (So not *that* much like Christmas but you know what I mean.)

Joan even drops me at the rollerskating rink in the afternoon (where I have a surprisingly good time with Amelia – I suppose I should stop being surprised by that now) *and* picks me up again.

On Saturday night Joan *insists* we order a takeaway pizza, then we have a family game of Twister (which Joan and I are the best at, but I win overall – thank you, thank you very much). Then we watch a film. It's the most fun I've had with my family since Dad went to live up a tree. Maybe even a little before he left.

"Thanks, Joan," my mum says quietly once Ryan is upstairs brushing his teeth for bed. I'm sitting in the chair nearest the television pretending not to be listening.

"You're welcome," says Joan loudly, not sensing my mum's tone. "See? It's like I always say, it's important to remember the fun things in life, isn't it?"

"Well, yes," says my mum at normal volume now. "But only sometimes. Kids do need routine and boundaries."

"But you guys *never* have fun!" cries Joan. "Your poor kids. Throw them a bone every now and then."

Yeah! I want to cheer. (But I know I'll be sent upstairs.) *Throw us a bone every now and then, Mum.*

I *love* it when Auntie Joan comes to stay.

The next day I feel so full from pizza that I'm not sure I can even face the Pop Tarts that we're now *definitely* allowed for breakfast. But I make a good go of it. I'm kind of a hero like that.

Now that I know Auntie Joan thinks my dad is "standing up for things" and not "crazy", I feel like I should really follow his example.

Hmmm. Am I standing up for what I believe in at school, I wonder? But how exactly can I do any more? I can't exactly *force* my friends to do the comic with me.

Maybe I there's another way I can get my point across? *Hmmmm.* I should play to my strengths. The only thing I've ever really been good at is drawing cartoons. They're my one super-power.

I remember when Tammy told me about the power of a satirical cartoon. I am going to draw a cartoon. Yes, I am!

I sit at my desk and think for a bit. Then I draw some sheep actors and actresses forgetting their roots and their friends now that they are famous. Oh, yes. Ha ha. I think I've made my point.

Don't mess with the best, cos you'll end up like the rest! (I would never say that in real life.)

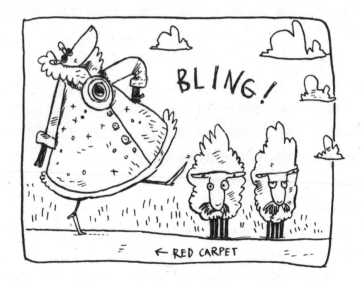

Chapter 19

At Monday's after-school rehearsal I march straight up to Joshua and Tanya and show them my satirical cartoon.

Joshua cracks a massive grin and Tanya laughs, then punches me on the arm (in a friendly way) but it's still enough to make me go flying for a second.

"OK, point taken," says Joshua. "We promise we will *definitely* put more effort into—"

"Hey, not *this* again!" Natalie marches over, looking upset.

"Calm down, luv," says Tanya.

Nat ignores Tanya for now and addresses me. "Have fun *rollerskating*, did you?"

"Yes, thanks," I reply. *As is my inalienable right as*

a free citizen, I don't add. (I told you I still know the word inalienable. You don't forget a thing like that in a hurry.)

"Well, I'm glad you and Amelia are having so much fun *without me*!" Nat yells, nearly crying. Then she storms off in the direction of the toilets.

I'm shocked by this outburst, but I follow Nat and see that she doesn't go into the toilets, she goes to the little nook under the stairs where there are some pegs for coats. She sits on a small table that has been left there, and cries.

Part of me feels terrible. I hate it when people cry, and obviously I feel somewhat responsible right now. But another part of me thinks: OK, let's try and sort this out. So, gingerly but determinedly, I approach Natalie.

"Hey … Nat?" I say gently.

Nat looks up and wipes her eyes with a tissue. "Oh," she says. "What do *you* want?"

I say the first thing that comes into my mind. "To bash you on the head with an inflatable hammer."

Natalie's surprise makes her burst out laughing, in

a slightly snotty way until she blows her nose with another tissue. It's much harder for her to be annoyed now that I've made her laugh. So far so good.

She smiles sadly at me and sniffs. "You think I've been unreasonable, then?"

"Oh *hell*, yes," I reply, which isn't very tactful of me, but it does make her laugh again.

I should probably try to remember my diplomacy but instead I say, "You've been an absolute *nightmare*." I sit next to her on the table. "What's going on?"

"Oh *Jess*!" Natalie flings her arms around me and cries into my neck. "I'm sorry." (At least I think that's what she says. Her voice is all high and crying-y.) I hug her back and try to comfort her, sort of patting her shoulder a bit.

"It's OK," I say. "Everything's going to be OK." That seems like the right thing to say. Of course I don't know what her problem is yet, but whatever it is, it's probably going to be OK.

We sit in silence for a bit while Natalie cries, then she stops crying so much and pulls away and blows her nose again. My neck feels wet from tears and (probably) snot, but I leave my arm around her instead of grabbing a tissue and wiping it. See — diplomacy!

"I don't know what's happened," says Natalie, wiping her eyes with another tissue. "I just felt under so much pressure with the musical. Like, I wanted it *so* much, and then I got it. And I couldn't believe it. And I thought that would make me happy. But it just made me really worried I'd mess it up. I've barely enjoyed any of it *at all*."

"You should have said something," I say.

"I said I was under pressure," says Nat.

"But you should have told me more how you were feeling. I'm an expert on this."

"Are you?" She looks at me quizzically.

"Yes," I insist. "OK. I know you'll laugh, or say it isn't the same, but that's how I feel every time I have to come up with a new comic idea."

"What?" Nat sounds a tiny bit scathing. "But you love your comic. That's all you talk about."

"Right," I say. "But every time I come up with a cartoon that people actually like, and think is funny or good, I think 'Oh no, that's it, I'll never draw a cartoon this funny again. They're going to hate my next one.'"

173

"But that's crazy," says Nat.

"I know!" I agree. "And then I sit at my desk and feel bad about myself, and feel like people are going to judge me. And *then*…" I pause for dramatic effect.

"What?" Nat prompts. Maybe I paused too long.

"And then, I think, 'Hey, you know what, it doesn't matter. I'm doing this for *me*. I'm just going to draw a cartoon that *I* find funny,' and then that magically frees me, and I can come up with all kinds of new ideas again."

"OK, I don't completely get how that applies to my situation," confesses Nat.

"So, you thought it would be fun to be in a musical because you love singing and dancing and performing? So do it for *you*. Because *you* love doing it. It doesn't matter what anyone else thinks. And you already know you're good because you got the part. Just enjoy it."

"Yeah," smiles Nat, processing this. "That's good advice, actually. Though it's easier said than done."

"Everything worth doing is," I reply sagely. (Either I made that up, or I heard Auntie Joan say it to Ryan yesterday about brushing his teeth.)

"Thanks," says Nat.

"Also, Amelia and I – but mainly Amelia – have been working really hard to make sure you get to do your really kick-ass Megan Flyer dance, so that really *will* be fun."

"That's another thing I've been feeling very low and insecure about," says Natalie.

"What?"

"You and Amelia," she says. "Going off together."

"See, that I *don't* understand," I say. "I thought you *wanted* us to be friends? You've spent loads of time *making* us hang out with each other."

"Yeah, but not without *me*."

"You do realise what a hypocrite that makes you, don't you?" I say.

"Yes," says Natalie guiltily. "I know we were way worse to you, but you know I'm sorry about that. And I would take it back if I could."

"Well, you really have nothing to be jealous of," I say. "We've only really bonded over how much we hate Harriet VanDerk." And I tell Nat all about Harriet, and how she kept being rude and controlling and tried to block the dance.

"I'm sorry," says Nat. "I was just being an idiot, and over-sensitive. I'm sorry I've been so over the top, Jess. Oh, it's so good to *talk* to you again."

"You, too," I say. "There's so much I've been dying to talk to you about." And then I tell Nat all about my dad going to live up a tree to save the forest and the birds.

"I just can't see your dad *doing* that," she finally says.

"*Tell* me about it," I say. "He's growing a beard and everything."

Nat splutters laugher. "I can't see your dad with a beard!"

"I know!" I agree. "But there you have it." I wonder how his beard is progressing, actually. Maybe I should go and visit him again.

"I'm so sorry I haven't been there for you, Jess. I promise I will be a much better best friend from now on."

"Thanks," I say. And we make our best-friend pendants match up briefly, like a little metal high-five, then laugh slightly at what idiots we are for doing it.

"So," I say. "Now that you're all happy and have stopped crying, would you like to see a cartoon of you as a diva sheep?"

Chapter 20

After school on Tuesday, Ryan, Lady and I make our way to the tree where my dad is currently living.

We go back past tents and protestors, the diggers, the ugly brown gash in the greenery, the workmen and the police (again, giving them a wide berth).

"Dad! Daaaaaad! Are you still up there? It's your children again!" shouts Ryan, as we approach Dad's tree. Lady barks as back-up.

"Kids? Ryan! Jessica?" My dad's excited voice shouts back. We look up at the tree and see the familiar but now much more beardy face peer over the edge of the tree house.

"Hi!" I call out, waving.

"Daddy! You *really* have a beard now!" exclaims Ryan.

"Yes, it's grown!" agrees my dad.

"How's it going?" I call up at him. "Still fun?"

"Well, I don't know about that!" calls back Dad. "But it's certainly *still important*. And that's why I'm doing this!"

"So you're still not coming down then?" I shout.

"Not yet!" comes the reply.

"Tammy came down," I shout. "Came and had a slap-up meal in our *proper* house!"

"I know. Who would have thought I'd be a better eco-warrior than Tammy!" My dad says this as if he's just won the best lawn competition or something.

"We miss you!" calls out Ryan. "It's very hard having a daddy who is also a hero." I think I hear Dad's beardy friend Jay laugh at that, but I can't see him.

"Auntie Joan is visiting!" I tell Dad.

"Oh yes?"

"She thinks this is the best thing you've ever done! She took us shopping and bought nice food."

"Well, that's good!" Dad replies.

"I wish you could come home," I say. "Mum's

upset you're using up all your holiday so now we can't go to Blackpool."

"Well, don't worry about *that*!" says Dad, suddenly sounding very far away and nothing like his old, responsible self.

"Um..." I begin.

"Things have a funny way of working out!" Now Jay's smiling and beardy face peers over the tree as well.

"When *are* you coming home?" I ask Dad.

"We just need to stay up here till the appeal goes through," answers Jay.

"That's assuming we win the appeal," says my dad.

"Oh, we will," says Jay confidently.

But what happens if they *don't*? Will they appeal again? Will Dad just have to stay up the tree indefinitely? It could go on *for ever*.

I thought it would be lovely to see my dad's familiar face and hear his calm, reassuring voice. But his face looks different, and his voice is saying uncharacteristically irresponsible things. *Hmmm.*

As Ryan, Lady and I arrive home, we see the VanDerks chatting to my mum across the little hedge in the front garden. *Here we go...*

"Hi, Mum," I say. "Hi," I mumble vaguely in the direction of the VanDerks.

"Hi, Mummy! Lady is thirsty, so I'm taking her inside for some water," says Ryan, going straight past.

"Oh, hello *Jessica*," sneers Mr VanDerk. "How's the preparation for the musical going? Heard about the song at the end."

"We've heard a few *interesting* things lately, haven't we, dear?" says Mrs VanDerk.

"Oh yes," chortles Mr VanDerk. "We've heard some *very interesting* things about the *protest* over the bypass too."

Uh-oh. They know. They know Dad is up a tree. This is Mum's worst nightmare about to come true. And they're really angry about whatever Harriet's told them, so they're going to use Dad as revenge. (*Honestly.* Sometimes I can't believe adults can be *so* immature.)

"It looks like it's going ahead," trills Mrs VanDerk

delightedly. "The bypass, that is."

"Yes, I can't see the appeal going in favour of the *nutcases*," agrees Mr VanDerk, allowing himself a chuckle.

"No offence," Mrs VanDerk adds quickly to Mum, and they chortle again.

"I don't know what you're talking about," pretends Mum.

"We know Bert's up a tree, protesting," says Mrs VanDerk. "It was in the paper."

"The cat's out of the bag!" wheezes Mr VanDerk.

"Don't worry, I'm sure he'll be home soon," Mrs VanDerk adds, mock-soothingly.

"And hopefully he'll just have to pay a *small* fine or something," adds Mr VanDerk. "I'm sure there'll be no jail time for dear old Bert."

"He's not breaking the law," says Mum.

"You keep telling yourself that," replies Mrs VanDerk.

"Poor old Bert. The stress finally got to him, eh?"

continues Mr VanDerk, smiling merrily. "You have to shape up or ship out in today's world. That's the harsh reality. I *am* sorry he's gone nuts, though," he adds, still smiling. (He doesn't look sorry at all, he looks delighted.)

"Well, I don't see what's so nuts about trying to protect the environment," says my mum defensively.

"No. Well, of course, it's *lovely* to have ideals," says Mrs VanDerk, faux-supportively.

"But progress always wins in the end," declares Mr VanDerk.

"I don't think the planet dying because there are no more trees is exactly *progress*," replies Mum.

"Well, of course you *would* stick up for him," says Mrs VanDerk, in a manner that suggests she understands a three-year-old's irrational obsession with a favourite blanket.

"I'm sorry?" says my mum.

"At least now we know where your Tammy gets it from!" simpers Mrs VanDerk and they both chuckle again.

"I must say, I wouldn't have thought it of him," says Mr VanDerk.

"I thought he had more sense than to get up a tree

at his age!" laughs Mrs VanDerk. "Still, I suppose it takes all sorts to be a hippy."

"My husband isn't *a hippy*," says my mum, angrily. "He's exercising his right to peaceful protest for a cause he believes in. He's an example of modern democracy in action. I'm delighted he's such a good role model for our children, showing that it's important to care about things other than money and getting a fifteen-minute lie-in!"

And with that, she grabs my hand, turns on her heel, and marches us back inside the house, slamming the door behind her.

"Having fun with the neighbours?" grins Joan as we storm into the kitchen.

"They're just *awful people*," mutters my mum, flicking on the kettle.

"Way to stand up for Dad!" I say, impressed. "Does that mean you've changed your mind about him staying up there?"

"I married him for better or for worse," says Mum. "And that includes him living up a tree if he likes."

She takes a sip of her tea and hands a cup to Joan. "It's just not the same as the way Bert makes it."

"Yeah, this is stewed," agrees Joan.

The three of us sit at the kitchen table, sipping drinks. (I've got Cream Soda – it's so amazing being allowed fizzy drinks!)

My mum can't stop reliving the VanDerks' jibes, even though she claims to not care what they think.

"I hope Bert *does* win the appeal, just to annoy them," she says finally.

"That's the spirit," I say, faintly sarcastically.

"It's not looking terrible," says Joan, who has the local paper in front of her. "It says here the appeal result will be announced in three days' time. So Bert just has to stay up there three more days, and then hopefully it will all be over."

"*Hmmm*," says Mum, sipping her tea and pulling another face.

"There's stuff we could do to help," says Joan.

"Like what?" asks Mum.

"All sorts," replies Auntie Joan, with a grin.

Chapter 21

"I can't believe I let you talk me into this," says Mum to Auntie Joan.

It turns out "all sorts" means doing an interview with the local paper, to offer the public "the human face" of the protest.

In keeping with Auntie Joan's views about positive action, Joan has suggested that our whole family be interviewed and photographed! It's all very nerve-wracking.

But that's not all! She's also been in touch with Horace King, and he's agreed to go on record giving his support to the protesters as well.

Within just twenty-four hours Joan has whipped up a media-storm! Well, kind of.

You know, *locally*. But *still*.

So on Wednesday after school (and chess club) we're all sitting on our sofa, smiling as a stranger takes photographs of us. (They actually requested Ryan and I wear our school uniforms – to show how local we are.)

And it's all going in tomorrow's paper. Just in time for the appeal.

They wouldn't let Ryan wear his space helmet, as they said it would "pull focus" from the issues. I think that's code for "look insane" but who am I to split hairs?

Ryan and I have been instructed to be on our best behaviour and to give positive answers whenever asked. We've just about managed it so far. But the journalist has been mainly talking to Mum. Then she turns to us.

"And why is this an important issue for you both?" she asks us.

I've got my answer ready. Auntie Joan coached us. "Because we like to play and walk our dog in the local area. There's so few *safe* places where we can do that now."

The journalist makes a special note of this. Auntie Joan said the key word was "safe". Lots of the other people reading this will be parents who worry about their children being *safe*, she said.

"Are you proud of your daddy taking a stand to protect the forest?" the journalist asks Ryan.

"My daddy is a hero," answers Ryan simply.

"Great. I think we've got all we need."

After they've gone, we turn on the TV and see Horace King on the regional news, talking to reporters at the site of the protest.

"Wow, you're good at this," I say to Auntie Joan.

"Hey, it's what I do for a living," she replies. "Well, kind of. Publicising an orchestra tour, helping save a forest – it's all in a day's work for me."

The next day the forest protest is front-page news! (Of our local paper.) There is a photograph of the tree houses and the diggers standing idle and under that a picture of Horace King with the caption: "Celebrities come forward to save Deanbury Forest."

Then in smaller writing underneath the caption, it says turn to page 2/4 for an interview with the family of one of the protesters... I turn the pages eagerly.

The headline reads, "Local father says 'No' to forest destruction" with a byline that reads, "Daddy is a hero," and then a smaller quote, saying "Protestors argue that the road is not necessary but the trees it would replace are."

There is the picture of the three of us, with another picture of Mum and Dad on their wedding day (the journalist wanted just a normal shot of Dad, but Mum said that was the only photo he looked good in, so they took a copy of it).

It's so weird, opening the paper and seeing my

family's faces staring back at me. But luckily I don't think the photo looks *too bad*.

Well, I guess people at school might hear about this now. *Hmmm*.

➡️

I haven't been bullied at all! And I've got through the whole day without anyone calling my dad a nutter. Quite the opposite, in fact. Lots of people have been joking that I'm famous now.

Tanya Harris berated me a bit for missing an opportunity to plug our comic. She said I should always have my "business head" on and never be "off duty". But to be honest, I think even if this had occurred to me at the time, I don't think the journalist would have included it. Not if they didn't want Ryan's space helmet in shot.

A few of the teachers have congratulated me on having such a caring and principled dad. Mrs Cooper even said, "Deanbury Forest is so beautiful, and some of those trees are so old. It's wonderful what your father is doing. I really hope they win."

I can't believe I've made it all the way to the after-school rehearsal without anyone taking the mickey. It's great.

Amelia and I have started teaching everyone the dance for the Megan Flyer number. It feels weird but fun. It's the big finale, so a lot of people need to know it.

Natalie is really good at it (obviously she sort of already knows it) which is really helpful for teaching the others. And everyone seems to be enjoying themselves.

Well, almost everyone. I've heard Harriet make a few nasty comments under her breath. We're just sort of ignoring her, though.

We stop the music again. "That's great, everyone," says Amelia happily. "Let's take it from the top again."

"Yeah, sure," mutters Harriet. "Really brilliant. I'd just dance my problems away if my dad was living up a tree."

Heeeeyyy, I think, annoyed. He's out of bounds. We had an agreement. But at least she's the only person who's bothered by it. Amelia and Nat glance at me, and I shake my head. It's not worth it.

"Hurry up and learn it, you lot, so we can get to my bit," says Tanya loudly. Then she does her witchy cackle again.

Tanya made it very clear that she didn't want to be in a pop song dance. So we've specially choreographed this extra bit in the middle, where she comes on and the group of dancers splits in two, sort of cowering as she walks through them. Then she does her own mini-evil dance, before everyone goes back to dancing together all happily. It's a stroke of genius on behalf of myself and Amelia, I think.

The music starts and we go through it again. It is getting better each time. I think. As we're dancing, Mrs Cooper approaches and stands behind Harriet to watch us.

When we stop the music again, Harriet (who obviously hasn't noticed Mrs Cooper) says louder this time, "That is the worst thing I've ever seen. Everyone looks like total morons. Especially Jessica."

"Harriet!" cries Mrs Cooper. "What a horrible

thing to say! We will not have this kind of negative disruption and bullying, thank you very much. Please go and stand in the corridor and wait for me there."

Harriet looks aghast. I'm not sure I've ever seen her be shouted at by a teacher before.

"Jessica," Mrs Cooper addresses me. "Do you know what this is about? Perhaps you had better go and stand in the corridor, too."

Oh *great*. I really hope a meal doesn't get made of this. I've done everything I can to limit everyone being mean to each other. It's not fair if it now looks like I'm Harriet's nemesis.

"Now, *what* is going on?" Mrs Cooper addresses both of us in the corridor as Megan Flyer continues singing inside the hall without us.

"Jessica has been very rude to me and difficult to work with," says Harriet.

What? "That's not true!" I cry. **WHAT?**

"And so has Amelia," Harriet adds, shamelessly.

"Wait here, please." Mrs Cooper goes back into the hall and reappears a moment later with Amelia. The music starts up again.

I love how our school suddenly cares loads about bullying *now*. When we've got a dance to teach.

Where were they when I was *actually* being bullied last term, eh? And why do they have to do this on *our* time?

"They've both been really nasty to me from day one," says Harriet. "They ganged up on me, and made my life really difficult."

"*What?*" cries Amelia. "Maybe in *opposite land*! You're the one that made everything difficult."

"When they got their own way with the dance, they mocked me and high-fived each other," continues Harriet.

OK, we did *kind of* do that. But not like that. Did we? No. I *hate* bullying. Harriet is twisting what happened so she sounds like the victim. And she picked on us *loads*. She *totally* sabotaged the paint. And she said I was really stupid!

"Mrs Cooper, Harriet is lying," says Amelia calmly, though she's obviously angry because she's gone a bit red. "She thought you had put her in charge of us, and she kept trying to boss us around and change what you'd told us to do."

"But I'm the *logical leader*," protests Harriet, giving herself away.

"'Logical leader'?" queries Mrs Cooper.

LOGICAL LEADER?

Honestly, Mrs Cooper could have nipped this all in the bud on *day one* if she'd just pointed out to Harriet that she wasn't in charge when she'd claimed she was. This is where politeness gets you.

"And Harriet was especially rude to Jessica and called her stupid in a very nasty way." Amelia is now just going for broke, it seems.

"Is that true, Harriet? Did you call Jessica stupid?" asks Mrs Cooper.

"Well, that's another thing I don't understand," says Harriet, ignoring the question. "Why was I given such boring, unimportant jobs to do? Why was so much favouritism shown to Jessica? Why did *she* get to draw all the pictures?"

"Oh my God, you're jealous!" cries Amelia. "Is that what all this has been about?"

"I'm cleverer than her," continues Harriet. "I'm *above* Jessica. I outrank her. Is it like a charity thing? Why doesn't this school reward intelligence?"

"*Harriet VanDerk*, that is an *extremely* nasty attitude you are displaying there," says Mrs Cooper curtly, suddenly looking very angry.

Harriet looks taken aback. She's not used to being told off by teachers.

"I don't care how clever you are in your other subjects, in my Art lessons and set design you are judged on your artistic skills. You can't buy your way in with good grades from other subjects, it doesn't work like that."

"Well, I don't see why not," huffs Harriet.

"You're not listening to me *at all*, are you, Harriet?" says Mrs Cooper.

"This is what she's been like the whole time, Mrs Cooper," says Amelia. "She thinks she's the best and she won't listen to criticism."

"She just somehow doesn't hear it," I add.

Her parents are the same. They just hear what they want to hear. That's why you can never really win an argument with a VanDerk, because they never realise that they've lost.

"All right, thank you, girls." Mrs Cooper obviously doesn't want us to just keep insulting Harriet. "I'm not happy with your attitude, Harriet. I think we might need to talk about that some more, in my office. But for the record, Jessica didn't get to draw *all* the pictures," says Mrs Cooper. "Lots of people did, including you."

"And Jessica's actually really good at drawing,"

says Amelia.

"I'm good at drawing, too," says Harriet.

"Jessica is better," says Amelia.

Harriet opens her mouth to protest but Mrs Cooper gets there first. "You don't have to be the best at *everything*, Harriet," says Mrs Cooper, not unkindly.

"*Yes ... I ... do!*" replies Harriet, bemused. "And I *am*."

"OK," says Mrs Cooper, experiencing for herself the brick wall that Amelia and I have lived with this whole time. "You two go back to the rehearsal," she addresses us. "Harriet, let's go to my office and have a chat."

Yeah, and I know how that chat's going to go, I think to myself as we walk back into the rehearsal. I almost feel sorry for Mrs Cooper. *Good luck.*

Chapter 22

It's so weird walking into the courthouse on the day of the appeal. (We're going to watch from the public gallery.) I guess I was expecting some kind of ye olde building or something, with big, intimidating décor and lots of fusty men in wigs (like on TV).

But our local county courthouse is surprisingly modern. There's no ye olde wooden floors, they're all a cheap and functional laminate. There's stark fluorescent lighting everywhere, and the whole place smells kind of like a leisure centre. I keep half expecting the judge to announce it's our turn next on the badminton courts.

The judge isn't doing that, though. He's barely said anything. (He is at least wearing a wig.) It's everyone else that's still droning on. I say *droning*, it's just a bit hard to understand what's going on.

It reminds me of when Auntie Joan took us to see Shakespeare, and it felt like it might as well have been in French, but I eventually managed to tune in a bit and understand more than a few snippets.

Joshua, Natalie and Amelia have come with my family to hear the results. Natalie is here to be supportive, Joshua *says* that's why he's here but I think he just wanted to see what it was like inside a courthouse. But at least him playing "thumb wars" with Ryan is stopping Ryan complaining about how bored he is.

This is taking longer than I thought it would. And it's hard to follow what's happening. It's like a really boring episode of *EastEnders*. Except no one can even be bothered to burst in and shout, "Woz goin on?" to cheer things up.

Basically, as far as I can tell, there's this environmental charity, "Green Fortis", (Fortis means warrior in Latin according to Auntie Joan). And they have a lawyer who keeps saying stuff. And then there's another lawyer "for the other side" who keeps saying stuff.

And then the Green Fortis lawyer guy says something about "presenting new evidence," and then someone gives a folder to the judge.

Then the judge says, "The road cannot go ahead. The area is the natural habitat of an endangered species. I hereby declare the appeal granted." And he taps a little hammer on his table.

Wait, what? That's good, isn't it? That's what we wanted to happen, *right*? I peer anxiously around at Joan and Mum.

"Yes!" shrieks Auntie Joan.

"Boo!" calls out a middle-aged man behind us.

Now it's more like *EastEnders*. Or the House of Commons. Or a panto.

"Come on," says Mum, standing up quickly. "Let's go and tell your dad!" She grabs Ryan's hand, and before I know it, we're speed walking out of the courthouse, with Amelia, Natalie, Joshua and I having to run slightly to keep up.

We go past some press on the steps outside, being told the news. But I don't catch what's being said.

To be honest, I don't really understand what's happening. But my Auntie Joan explains it to me as we walk.

The protesters were "buying time" so that the conservationists from Green Fortis could check the forest to see if it was home to any rare wildlife that was protected by law.

It was a longshot, but eventually they found some great crested newt breeding ground. And they are a protected species, which, according to Auntie Joan, meant certain statute laws kicked into action. Anyway, that's why the judge had to say the bypass couldn't be built there.

As we arrive at the site, we realise the press have beaten us to it and the protesters have all already come down from the trees to start celebrating. We spot Dad and start running towards him. He sees us and waves, but seems unsteady on his feet. I guess he hasn't used his legs properly for a bit.

Mum runs up and gives Dad a massive hug, while some camera flashes go off; then she immediately takes a step back, and I realise why: Dad smells really quite bad.

"Daddy's a hero," says Ryan proudly.

"A hairy, stinky hero," I add.

"That's not very nice, Jessica," says Mum, though I'm pretty sure her eyes are watering from the smell.

"Great to see you, Dad," I say. "I would hug you, but, you know…" I trail off.

"That's quite all right!" Dad beams. "Your mother was the canary in the cage for that one. I must get out of these clothes and have a bath."

"Congratulations, Bert!" says Auntie Joan, shaking Dad firmly by the hand despite the horrible smell. "I've never been more delighted that you married my sister."

"What about when the kids were born?" asks Dad.

But before Joan can explain why it sounds like she prefers trees to us, Tammy comes running over. "There you are!" she cries. "Don't forget to congratulate me, too." Tammy doesn't smell *at all*.

"Oh yes," I say. "What did you do again? 'Errands' and eating-pasta duty, wasn't it?"

Tammy pulls a sarcastic, *very funny* face at me, then goes back to trying to make herself look important.

"I mean, the thing is," she says grandly, "when you've lived up a tree like Dad and I have, it changes you, you know."

I cough-say the word "Nonsense" and Tammy frowns at me. Funny how now she *wants* to be lumped into the same group as Dad.

Some journalists want to take pictures of our whole family before Dad is allowed to get changed and have a shower, so we have to try and smile while smelling the worst smell any of us has ever smelled. I think we might all be grimacing in the photos, but what can you do?

A few feet away from us the man I recognise as Jay Bowman is talking to some journalists.

"I knew our people would be able to find the newts, and they did. It's a huge relief. It's a fantastic organisation and a great team. I would like to thank everyone involved..." Yeah yeah, whatever.

"Bert," says Mum. "You'd better call work and tell them you'll be back right away."

"No need," says Dad dismissively. "There's no panic. I've been offered another job anyway."

"By who?" asks Mum.

"None other than Jay Bowman." Dad beams.

"*Who?*" asks Mum.

"That guy." I point at the bearded and bedraggled man talking to the press.

Mum scrutinises Jay Bowman. I think it's fair to say that his appearance doesn't fill her with confidence.

"Did I hear my name?" Jay smiles and waves at

204

us. Mum automatically waves and smiles politely back, but you can tell she secretly doesn't think this venture has "success" written all over it.

Chapter 23

"OK," says Tanya, as we all sit on the comfy chairs outside the library at lunchtime. (Finally the gang is back together again for the comic meetings.)

"Who votes for the Parents' Handbook to be a free separate little booklet with the next issue? Say 'Aye'."

"Or raise your hands," says Lewis. "Probably easier to raise your hands."

"Or whistle," I joke. "Let's make this interesting."

"Enough," interrupts Joshua. "Separate booklet, raise your hands?"

We *all* raise our hands.

"What was the point of this vote again?" I ask, laughing.

"I was against it, but I've changed my mind," explains Lewis.

"Marvellous," I say.

"OK, on to other business," says Tanya. And then we have the never-ending debate about whether we should raise the price of the comic again. *Ahh*. It's good to be all back together. *Hmmmm.*

Although in some ways, I think Lewis and I sort of got more done without these clowns. *Ha ha*, I just called Tanya and Joshua clowns in my head, and they'll never know. I giggle.

"What?" asks Joshua.

"You're a bunch of clowns," I reply happily. OK. So maybe they *will* know. "It's good, though," I say, as they look at me like I'm odd. "Clowns are funny. You know, we're a good, funny team."

"Whevs," says Tanya, but I'm pretty sure she's flattered.

I'm glad we're all back together again, though. Because Joshua, Tanya and I have also started work on the sequel to the Parents' Handbook, the Teachers' Handbook. And coming up with stuff for that has helped take my mind of my family.

Dad hasn't managed to wash the crazy right out of his hair yet. Or shave it right out of his beard yet. (Although he has shaved and washed and he no longer smells.) And he still hasn't gone back to work yet.

As I arrive home from school and step over a barking Lady (probably in both senses of the word) I find she has been chewing something and there are bits all over the hall floor. Oh *nooooo*. We were doing so *well*. At least it's just a free paper that no one ever looks at.

Still, now I have to hide the evidence before Mum tells Lady off. I'm just pondering whether I should even throw it away a few doors down because

Mum sometimes goes through the bins to check we're recycling properly, when I spot a familiar name in a headline.

" 'Jay Bowman Strikes Again'," I read. *Eh?*

Then my eyes find their way to the picture. *Is that...?* Surely not. Is that clean-shaven, successful-looking man the same Jay Bowman that I met living up a tree with my dad?

I read on. "Jay Bowman has secured another victory for his environmental charity, Green Fortis..." Whoa. Wait, *his* charity? I scan the rest of the page. "...Green Fortis came to fame by making and selling recycled paper and other goods ... gone from strength to strength ... branched out into other areas ... ethical chocolate ... electric cars ...  preservation... Founder Jay Bowman has said he is delighted..." *Founder.* It *is* his charity!

Oh my *God*, Dad has been offered a job by a bonafide successful environmentalist. He could have a proper new job after all! One he actually likes! Everything's going to be OK!

I stroke Lady. "Good dog, Lady. You're a genius. Or at least, half a genius."

"Why is she half a genius?" asks Ryan, walking past and completely accepting this as a thing.

I check Mum's not around then show Ryan the paper. "Quick! Hide it!" he says, alarmed.

"It's OK, I'm going to put it in Number Thirty's recycling," I say. "The thing is, this shows that Dad has been offered a new job by a proper man. We won't lose the house when he inevitably gets fired from his current job for never turning up to work."

"OK," says Ryan, not looking that impressed by my revelation.

"If Lady didn't chew stuff I would never have seen it," I add. "So in that way, she's a genius."

"But surely she would only be a genius if she *knew* what that paper said?" Ryan is troubled by my logic. "But she didn't."

"*Didn't* she, Ryan?" I ask, trying to sound wise. "*Didn't ... she?*"

Ryan sighs, as if I am wasting his time. "Please don't chew anything else, though, Lady," he implores, stroking her.

Lady responds by rolling over so that her minions (us) can stroke her stomach for her. Ryan immediately kneels down to do so.

"See?" I say. "Genius."

"Hi, Jessica," says Harriet VanDerk at the next rehearsal after school. Amelia and I are painting in the red on the poppy-fields canvas. We're both a bit startled that she's come over to us.

"Uh, hi," I reply. It's awkward. I haven't spoken to her since she tried to get me in trouble and then asserted that she deserved to rule supreme over us all because she's the cleverest person in the world.

"I, uh, wanted to apologise," says Harriet. *What?* Well, this is genuinely a first. "For being rude to you during the set design."

"Um." What can I say? The only polite thing *to* say is: "Um, that's … OK." *Is it though?* Is it OK? And this is so unlike Harriet.

"I think I showed bad management," she clarifies. OK, still going with this *in charge* thing, I think. That's a bit more like Harriet.

"I had a good chat with Mrs Cooper," continues

Harriet. (Poor Mrs Cooper.) "And she actually gave me a leaflet about getting on with people." (A *leaflet?*) "And so I would like to say to you, Jessica, you are quite good at drawing." (Quite good? *Quite?*) "And I would like to work with you in the future."

Ah, *I see*, she wants to *excel* at getting on with people. That's her new challenge. Oh well, that's better than nothing. Quite clever of Mrs Cooper to channel her ambition and competitiveness into something harmonious and productive, I guess.

"OK, Harriet," I say politely. "That sounds great."

Harriet beams and looks at Amelia. "And you too, of course, Amelia." She adds this a bit reluctantly.

Amelia looks like she is about to say something nasty, but she glances at me, and then says, "Fine." Also, quite reluctantly.

"Great!" says Harriet. "So I had some ideas about

when the snow falls on the poppies," and just like that, Harriet is trying to be a *team-player.*

Amazing.

Chapter 24

So. What has two thumbs and an opening night of the musical that they designed the set for? *This guy!* (You can't see me, but I am pointing at myself, with my thumbs.) Oh yes.

The set looks amazing! *Naturellement.* (That's French for *naturally*, fact fans.) As in, it's a natural fact that I am amazing at set design. (And still modest too, of course.)

Finally – the moment of truth. The musical! Well, if I told you it goes really well … I'd be *underselling* us! It's phenomenal! (Obviously mainly the set, but I think the acting helps a *bit*.) Ha ha.

The dance we taught everyone is brilliant. It makes for an amazing feel-good ending. Plus it comes as a massive surprise. Because the rest of the musical is more traditional in tone (with the odd joke added) the modern music starting up at the end is kind of eclectic.

The music starts and the audience actually start up a rhythmical handclap. Amazing. Everyone knows the dance perfectly. Tanya plays it for laughs just perfectly. The audience *love* her bit. I'm pretty sure her family start wolf-whistling too.

When we finish, we get a standing ovation from the audience! Who are, admittedly, mainly our parents but *still*. It's such an amazing feeling. Especially for me, who has never danced in public before, and probably never will again.

"So, kids," says my mum, as we arrive climb out of the car in front of the house, and after I have been given the required amount of praise.

"There's something we need to tell you," says my dad.

"Oh, yes, I'm all ears," I say. I'm feeling quite happy because of all the praise I've been receiving.

"You know your dad's new job," says Mum. Of course we do. My dad has the *best job ever*. It is literally the best job I've *ever* heard of *anyone* doing.

My dad now works for Green Fortis, which is a green and ethical company with its own charity, trying to raise awareness of various environmental issues.

BEST JOB EVER

Guess what one of those issues is? *Chocolate.* Green Fortis are involved in "smart" farming that doesn't destroy land and provides fair wages for the people involved.

My dad gets free chocolate! From his company. He goes in to work, and then he comes home, with oodles of *free* ethical chocolate. The only better job would surely be working in a chocolate factory itself.

I one hundred per cent endorse and stand by Dad's courageous decision to follow his dreams, no matter what. I  think the lesson we have all learned here is that doing that will always end well, probably with free chocolate for everyone.

"Well, part of working there involves *going green*," my mum is saying.

"Yeah, yeah, we know," I say. "We love the ethical chocolate. We should get ethical everything."

"Great, I knew you'd be on board," says my dad. "We're going to have an ethical car. It's being delivered tonight." As my dad says this we approach our front door and my mum gets her keys out.

"What's an *ethical* car?" I ask. (A *horse*? Surely that would be cruel…)

"An electric car," says my dad.

"Cool, like a space car!" says Ryan.

It is at this point that our new car is delivered. The electric-ness of the car is brilliant and fine and I don't with a problem with it.

But the car *itself* is a bright, lime-green colour. In fact, it's almost luminous. And it has a slogan on the side in big, bright yellow writing (so it almost looks like it's advertising a tropical juice drink).

Except it says

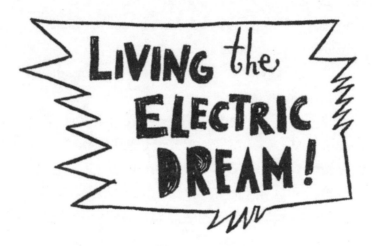

Which kind of makes it sound like a statement about a preferred choice of music, rather than an environmental cause. Or like my dad is in a band from the 80s or something.

OK. I might have to take back some of what I said about Dad's job being *perfect*. I should have known there'd be a catch. Dammit.

Hmmm. This might be the living end. It's probably not. But it *might* be.

Acknowledgements

Thank you to Kate Wilson and everyone at Nosy Crow for taking a chance on an unknown kid, and publishing me.

Thank you to Suzy Jenvey for believing in my work, and taking it to Nosy Crow.

Thank you to Lindsey Fraser and Kathryn Ross for supporting me over books two and three, and having fun in Edinburgh.

A massive thank you to Kirsty Stansfield for being a fantastic editor, and Dom Kingston for making every book event non-scary and so joyful.

Thank you to Sarah Horne for drawing such fantastic illustrations that I love and are perfect.

Thanks to all my family and friends who don't mind if I ignore them and spend weeks in my pyjamas covered in crisps when I am finishing a book.

And finally, thank you to every reader who has enjoyed these books, and told a friend, made a nice comment, or helped spread the word.